The True Tale of Santa the Zombie Slayer

Will Luckman

The True Tale of Santa the Zombie Slayer by Will Luckman

Published by William Luckman.
https://willluckmanwrites.wixsite.com/willluckman

willluckmanwrites@gmail.com

Cover design by Rafael Batista Da Silva.
https://rafahstrife.artstation.com

Chapter Header Images sourced from and modified with, express permission of Clipart.com

It took many hands to make this work.

My mother taught me to dream.
My father taught me to persist.
My wife gives me strength.
My kids make me proud.

Thank you all for making this dream come true. Now on to the next adventure.

Contents

Prologue

Twas the night before Christmas and all through the house, just one creature did stir as he chewed on a mouse. Now his eyes shot with red and some blood on his chin, this zombie had just killed the family within. Like an eager young child such a clatter he rose, as he'd torn open presents from heads down to toes. And though now as he gobbled his victims down fast, he should savor this meal for it may be his last.

A new hero was coming to vanquish this plight, slaying zombies so all could enjoy Christmas night...

1

SEASON'S EATINGS

A delicate chill crackled through the skies as frozen butterflies danced in the night—with each icy ember sparkling on its journey downward while a light blanket of snow gently tucked the town in for its silent yuletide slumber. It was a scene so picturesque in its snow globe-like serenity were it not for the rabid monster indulging its secret feasts of flesh in the shadows like a guilty vegan.

Of course, this place sucked long before the zombie wrapped its lips around some locals. Ironically, a touch of death was one of the livelier events it had seen in quite a while.

Outside the shredded shutters of the ransacked abode, scattered streetlamps did their best to brighten the mood, though long shadows still dulled the vibrant blue and yellow box-like homes that fringed the sidewalk. Greenland may have only been a stone's throw from the North Pole, but if you were hoping to squeeze even a drop of Christmas spirit from this joyless wasteland, good luck—she was bone dry.

Suddenly, as the clock edged an hour closer to midnight, the soft jingle of sleighbells began to echo off an old stone wall, growing louder and faster with each jolly shake. An ancient wooden door soon swung open with a creak, and an old man stepped into the street, searching for that magical sound.

He stood for a moment, shielding his dilated pupils from the streetlight as they adjusted from the grimy shithole where he'd spent the past few hours pouring drinks.

The sound was unmistakable, and when his straining gaze soon found its mark, the emotion of what his eyes beheld could not be contained as he began wildly waving his arms to grab their attention.

"Hey," he growled gruffly. His lips parted and chest heaved, giving every ounce of strength to ensure he was heard. "Get out of here, you horny mongrels!" the old man bellowed as he swept up a half-frozen bucket of water from the snow and tossed it over some local strays who were taking the mistletoe tradition a few bases too far. They yelped as they barreled off down the street, the female's tattered old collar still jingling as they faded into the distance.

The barman shook his head as he watched the dogs disappear and took this opportunity to casually wedge a finger down the back of his pants, letting it wander the aisle like a pensioner at a garage sale. The lonely probe soon found its mark as a loose nail caught a boil that had been festering for days, dragging a trail of pus along his fingertip that proved delightfully gross when inspected upon the mandatory sniff.

The painful euphoria brought a grin to his weathered jaw, as he grabbed the crooked handle of the door and heaved the squeaky hinges back into the throngs of servitude. The old man mumbled to himself, more out of habit than any lingering irritation, as he hobbled back inside where Santa was causing a ruckus.

WHERE THERE'S SMOKE THERE'S FIRE... AND DRAGONS AND ZOMBIES

After his brief stroll, the old man wandered back into the ruins of his crumbling, centuries-old farmstead that now housed a few barrels of beer, an old sheep pen-turned-boxing ring, and a steady flow of drunk locals and Norwegian traders looking for some downtime. The place was a dump, but the Inuit loved its rustic charm over the imported, color-coded boxes that were now popping up all over the land since Denmark brought the modern age to their shores. The 'perks' of the colonial life, apparently.

Slap!

The sweaty smack of fist on skin echoed across the crowded room as if swinging from the rotting rafters. Within the walls of this unassuming sanctuary, a 30-something year old Santa was enjoying a rather easy night in the ring—onto his third opponent, with this one already on the ropes. In fact, the poor guy was quite literally entangled in the tattered ringside ropes, and you could get even-money odds that there were more of his teeth in the coagulating dirt than remained in his head.

Thud!

A shot to the abdomen buckled his challenger who sucked a long wheezing breath into his winded lungs. Of course, watching Santa beat ass might seem a little less festive than tucking a present under your tree, but that's because this guy *wasn't* Santa. Not yet anyway. It was years before the King of Christmas would assume his throne—before that, at some point, people just called him Claws, and his life was in the ring.

Whack!

Claws swung his mighty fist across the jaw of his wobbling foe, spewing blood from his shredded lips with the force of a sprinkler dousing a lawn. Like a crop of daisies, the crowd surged under the falling red raindrops, while among them, a pale man in a trenchcoat slowly worked the room. He was popping into conversations, whispering in ears and just generally talking up his client.

"Careful ladies," the man warned some young women as he casually leaned his back against a pole, never breaking his gaze from his man in the ring. "I heard this guy is the last of the great Viking warriors that once ruled these lands," he gossiped, "and trained in their merciless arts before his ancestors vanished into the snow." He disappeared as the women's jaws dropped in awe.

"Did you know he is undefeated in 100 fights?" he quizzed two old drunks, one of whom looked considerably displeased at the news, since he had thrown a sizeable bet behind the other guy.

After dodging a swinging fist, the trenchcoated whisperer then took a seat down at another table full of roaring young gents. "Yep, the Polar Punch they call him," he sat right in the middle of the group to avoid further repercussions from the old, angry drunk guy. "I heard he once took down a charging polar bear with a single right hook. That's where he got his fur coat."

Crack!

One of the young gents punched the air with his beer hand, and cheered as Claws took another hefty swing at his opponent who had rallied late in the round. As more drops of blood sailed across the room onto his forehead, this only served to heighten the young man's manic aggrandizement. It also didn't bode well for the mug in his hand, which was now being shaken free from its last vestiges of liquid. As the beer began raining down on the table, the trenchcoated man beat a hasty retreat in disgust to begin wiping the fresh puddles of alcohol from his sleeve. That was enough mingling for tonight.

Whether true or not, his stories had purpose, often proving a useful tool for his client in the ring, as just a swing of that fabled arm was enough to reap cries of surrender from many a foe without ever landing a shot. Of course, others took the great myth as a challenge, and Claws' body was well hardened from many epic clashes with such aspiring thugs. But that was *his* job. We each play to our skills.

With the hapless foe soon locked under his arm, Claws was just reaching for a beer as he chatted up a particularly, shall we say, perky young lass in the crowd, when a scorching hot woman burst through the doors—out of breath and screaming for help. She was an Inuit local, not a day over 30, with black hair and piercing eyes that seemed to capture his soul when she flashed him a glance. He was paralyzed.

Naturally every man rose to attention when she marched in the door, most without leaving their seat, ready to give her their best until one word set them back down in a unified retreat. "Dragon!"

A giant fire-breathing monster had descended upon her home. Last she saw, her father was battling the beast alone while her mother scrambled to gather the kids.

This young woman was blackened and burnt, and it seemed the adrenaline of the night was the only thing keeping her going. She waited a moment—more to catch her breath than in any hope of a show of chivalry—then turned and stumbled back out the door.

Claws looked across the room at the cowards around him and sneered. Suddenly, a fist bumped his jaw, and Claws turned to see his opponent waiting with knuckles raised looking unconvincingly tough in the middle of the ring. He angrily picked up his opponent and hurled him out of the arena before grabbing his coat and marching to the door. The man flew across the room and smashed into the scoreboard, ironically rubbing his own name off the board as his battered face slid to the floor.

The stunned barman offered Claws a bag of gold as he passed—prize money for his many victories that night—but the champ raised a hand, rejecting the offering. "Not this time, Joe. I've found someone bigger to fight," he called out as he stepped onto the street to follow his damsel in distress.

The pale man in the trenchcoat, who had been enjoying the one-sided contest, suddenly turned a lighter shade and dived towards the barman's outstretched hand. Disgusted by Claws' refusal of the winnings, he ripped the pouch of gold coins from the beer handler's mitt and hurriedly tucked it into his pocket as he shuffled out the door.

"Why is it you always find a way to refuse the scraps these troglodytes try to throw at you?" he called out to the victor, who was now standing in the snowy street watching the young woman return to her home. This settlement looked so different to the way Claws remembered it being as a child. Where beautiful huts of driftwood and bone once dotted the shoreline, he now gazed across a rainbow of colorful timber homes that stood in their place.

He looked ahead at the target, following a trail of smoke downward to an old stone church on the edge of town where the young woman and her family had taken residence. Masked in smoke, it crackled like a lightning storm each time the dragon within would blast its flame, and each thunderous roar saw more of the crumbling walls abandon ship and hurl themselves into the dirt as if to escape the inferno.

Much like the bar Claws had just left in his wake, this was one of the centuries-old structures built when powerful Viking tribes once ruled the land—his ancestors, if the rumors were to be believed. Claws had been listening to Morty's sales pitch for so long he couldn't remember *who* he was anymore. He could have been anyone from the son of Odin to a homeless drifter.

In any case, those tribes were long gone, and the stones had worn. It seemed the moss and twisted vines were the only things holding this place together. If the dragon didn't destroy it, time had a finger waiting on the trigger anyway.

"We'd be rich by now if we actually started accepting your winnings," Morty whined with just the right level of shrill demand to drag Claws back from his trance.

"Look, Morty, I make the rich pay their dues, but these people can barely afford to feed themselves, let alone line the pockets of a stranger." Claws was resolute in his stance, clearly deeper in thought than the idle chit-chat his manager was insisting upon.

"What stranger? You're a regular here. They love you." Mortus was working Claws' ego like an oily masseuse, and knew just where to push to maintain control. He may not have been as physically gifted as his muscle-bound meal ticket, but Mortus had a few extra years of experience on this Earth, and was smart enough to know there was more than one way to win a fight.

"They love to watch me fight. Don't mistake that for affection. It could be any man there in that ring and still they would cheer. I'm as common as vermin to them. A nobody."

Mortus sensed a new determination in Claws' voice and swiftly acted to soften his stance. "Hey, now, that's no way for my prize-fighting bull to be talking. You're a hero," he said, then solemnly concluded, "You're *my* hero."

"Beating up natives is not heroic. Being a hero takes something..." Claws returned to the trail of smoke winding skywards in the distance. He saw the woman stop at the house and look back to where he stood, watching him, and waiting. This was his moment, he felt it. "... greater," he concluded.

Finishing his musings, he took a moment to process the gravity of his intentions. Sure, he could dream of heroism and adventure, but now it was staring him right in the face. The question was, would he dare? Call it destiny, fate, or quite simply a rush of blood to his briefs, but as the sweat dripped down the panting chest of his waiting damsel, he felt compelled to at least go check her out. *It* out. Check out her... situation. *Nice save*, he thought to himself, with a satisfied grin.

He locked onto his target and ran towards the blaze, calling back to his friend. "Sorry Morty, I've got to do this. And don't worry about the money. I'll pay you back the next fight I get. Wish me luck, old friend."

By now Morty had already lost interest in their conversation and was secretly counting the gold. He knew that Claws would do whatever he wanted anyway. He just rolled his eyes and mumbled quietly to himself insincerely. "No, don't go, stay here, I can't survive without you. Pff!" he chuckled to himself at his client's naivety before wandering after him. "Imbecile!"

Claws arrived at the house in no time and found the scaly winged reptile on the roof, pacing across it while raining flames down on the occupants. Screams came from inside as the family tried to escape. He could see the father around the rear of the house, hitting the beast with a shovel. *Not the most logical weapon of choice*, thought Claws, but in the heat of the moment he guessed anything was better than nothing.

Claws ran to the father's aid, dodging some falling debris on the way. The old man was transfixed on his opponent and didn't notice Claws approach. Claws put a hand on his shoulder to check on him, but when the father spun around it was not a look of surprise or fear on his face. His eyes instead, were bloodshot, his mouth twisted in a sneer. There was a mix of blood and rabid spittle glistening on his lips, and his breathing was heavy and fast. This had been a busy night for the old man. He had only just made it home from his feeding frenzy across town before this dragon popped in for a snack of its own. Now most people like to follow a big meal with a little siesta, but here he was trying to defend his family while another was still rolling around in his stomach.

The father let out a growl and struck Claws in the chest before turning and running into the forest. The stunned hero had little time to consider the moment as a giant tail suddenly flicked past his face, knocking out another section of the house.

Claws dived out of the way and quickly scanned for a weapon. The dragon was watching him now and swatted again with its tail. This one caught him off guard and slammed him into a wall. Briefly dazed, he grabbed the shovel and swung it hard at the tail—the blade slicing through the dragon's thick hide as it roared in pain. OK, so maybe the old man wasn't completely bat-shit crazy. This thing wasn't bad.

Claws spun the shovel effortlessly to block the attacks as the dragon continued to lash out with its tail like a cat chasing a mouse. Clearly it still didn't consider him enough of a threat to even bother turning around, but with every slice of his oddly effective blade, it would draw the occasional glance from the beast and was chipping away at its patience. He felt kind of dumb putting so much effort into just defeating the tail, and this was doing no favors for his confidence about taking on the rest of the beast.

Just then the tail swept low, forcing Claws to leap over it, and before his feet could touch down again, it came back and knocked him well across the ground. He groaned with some definite bruising creeping into his rib cage. While he had been doing well fending off the tail, at this rate he'd be dead before he got within arm's reach of its asshole.

He needed a new plan.

Finally, Morty arrived—at a leisurely pace—at the front of the house. Looking in, he could see Claws wincing in pain on the ground and considered helping. He even took one step towards the fray, but after nearly losing his footing on a wobbly board he threw out his arm to steady himself, grazing a sooty wall with his fingertips. He grumpily shook his head as he looked at the blackened ash on his hand and wiped his fingers on his coat as he retreated.

Back in the yard Claws climbed to his feet and spotted a pitchfork nearby. He quickly grabbed the gardener's trident and slammed it down on either side of the dragon's tail. It wouldn't hold long but he would take whatever he could get at this point just to try and generate a thought. Then Claws noticed a bucket of water on the ground that the father must have prepared earlier to douse the flames. A long chain ran from the handle, which Claws gathered in one hand while keeping the shovel in the other. Looking up he could see the beast was still on the other side of the house, but had now set its gaze on him as it tried to wriggle its tail free of the trap.

Quickly setting the shovel just above the tip of the dragon's tail, Claws stomped down as hard as he could to sever the end. This sent the beast into a rage as it ripped the pitchfork from the ground and made its way toward him.

"Well, now that I've got your attention..." Claws smiled mockingly as the beast twisted awkwardly on the weakening stone pillars of the house.

As he waited for the retaliation, Claws began slowly swinging the bucket in a circle around his body, gaining momentum with every rotation and raising higher up his torso, kind of like the swinging chair ride at carnivals if these had been invented yet. Soon the centrifugal force of the swing took effect and the water sat firmly in the bucket. He began to let out the length of the chain further until the bucket was swinging far around and above his head.

With the roof collapsing beneath it, the dragon at last stretched out its gigantic wings and leapt across the roof, landing almost on top of Claws with its mouth wide and fire rising in its throat. No sooner did it land, than Claws put all his might into one final swing, sending the bucket crashing into its head with water cascading down its throat to extinguish the flames. The creature coughed for a moment as it tried to ignite the gas rising in its gorge, but the water had soaked the stony textured gland responsible for throwing out a spark. So, with the beast incapacitated, Claws breathed a sigh of relief and sat back on the ground.

He took a deep breath and smiled to himself. Sure, the house was destroyed, but he had certainly done some good by subduing the beast. He was a hero, and with any luck that young woman he just saved had a bucketload of gratitude waiting to repay him. Claws enjoyed, for a brief moment, playing over in his mind the many amazing—and quite probably sexual—ways she might repay him before it slowly dawned on him that he'd just been fighting a dragon, and the ten-thousand-pound reptile had far more to offer in its arsenal than just a bit of hot air.

3

DO YOU FEAR WHAT I FEAR?

Just then a shadow began to descend upon Claws, and the giant beast looked him square in the eyes. Claws froze in place. Even the reflexive motion of his eyelids dared not to flutter as the vision of his waiting executioner blurred through his drying eyes.

He took a slow step back, but the wall of the neighbor's abode blocked his retreat. He was trapped. Remaining still, he scanned the scene for another weapon but, alas, the garden shed was all cleaned out of lethal weaponry unless he could find a more offensive use for some slow-roasted pot plants.

He took a step left but the beast blocked his path. He moved right and so, too, did it follow. Then it opened its massive jaws in a rumbling growl. This was normally the part where the flames of hell would spew from its gob and char him into the human equivalent of a raisin... but nothing happened. It seemed the water had *indeed* dampened its natural ignition switch. All Claws could feel and smell was the hot volatile gas in the creature's breath, but missing the key ingredient that made things go BOOM, so instead it just burned all the way down into his lungs, causing his injuries to sizzle and sting.

"Oh, ho, hoooo," he coughed, with the chesty depth of a pack-a-day smoker.

Through the smoke, Claws caught a glimpse of Morty standing by. His friend seemed surprised and somewhat angry to learn he'd been spotted and reluctantly made his way onto the property again to help—moping like a teenager nagged into doing the chores. Of course, the moment Claws' attention was diverted, Morty quickly ducked away and hid again. He was not a fighter, and was open to all forms of cowardice and deception to avoid the heat of battle. Morty would do anything for his friend, but not at the expense of his own safety, comfort, or indifference to the task. Claws knew this. *If anything*, Morty decided, *he should be the one to blame for not remembering that.*

Claws looked back up at the impotent flamethrower as it readied to lunge for the final blow. He closed one eye and braced for impact, his end as apparent and unglorified as the piece of tobacco he'd not long spat into the dirt. But before the beast could strike, three arrows came in rapid succession from the darkness, striking the dragon in the temple and killing it instantly. The reptile collapsed on top of the house, its mighty head coming to rest just an inch from Claws' feet.

Still stunned, he scanned for his savior and noticed the young woman standing with her bow still poised at the front of the house. She smiled, though her eyes remained on the beast.

"Nice work, Muscles. You make a pretty useful distraction," she cooed proudly.

Claws stood for a moment, still processing the bizarre chain of events. Between the aggressive monstrousness of the father; his first encounter with a dragon; and being rescued by this 'damsel in distress', it had been a pretty stressful night. He took a deep breath to calm his nerves, but once again his lungs burned as if on fire. "Oh, ho, hoooo," he coughed.

"Sounds like someone can't handle a little smoke," the young woman quipped as she began clambering over the debris toward him. "Hey, Princess, I thought you came here to save the day. What happened?" she teased.

"I... I was getting to it," stammered Claws, his response far from convincing.

"Forget it, I just saved *your* life. You owe me one now," she said, looking pleased with herself.

"Thanks?" he replied sarcastically with considerable discomfort in his voice—partly from the burning gas in his lungs but more so because his dreams of hero sex were fading faster than the flames.

The woman climbed the final hurdle of rubble and landed next to Claws. "Not very convincing but I'll take it. So how is my little damsel in distress?" she asked.

Damn, she'd used his line against him. Claws gathered himself at last and responded more confidently. "I had it covered. You know you're not very grateful considering I gave up a considerable purse to come and save your family."

"You're right," she shot back. "And maybe I should have offered to hold it for you while you cowered in..."

Suddenly her eyes widened, and fear engulfed her face as she remembered.

"My family!" she exclaimed.

Without a thought of self-preservation, she ran inside the smoldering house and flitted frantically from room to room, tossing aside burning furniture—her adrenaline blocking the pain of her scalding palms.

"Mom? Aggy?" she called desperately, her voice strained through panic and toxic fumes.

Claws followed when suddenly Mortus stepped out of the shadows, looking relieved. "Finally, I found you my fr...," he began.

"Not now, Morty," ordered Claws, as he brushed his friend aside and continued into the house. Mortus was oblivious to his haste, more irritated, in fact, by their dismissal of him, despite the selfless effort he'd made to finally venture so far into the hazardous battle zone.

"Can you fetch my gloves from the bar?" Claws called back. Mortus scowled as he watched Claws disappear into the rubble. Fetch his things? *What do I look like, a dog?* Mortus sighed to himself, then headed back up the street—the things he did for this guy. *He* was the *real* hero.

Claws dodged a flaming beam as it dropped from the ceiling, and vaulted a table that now just seemed a pile of ash. After a short search he found the woman standing in the middle of the house, looking into the remnants of one of the rooms. A pile of burning beams had collapsed in the corner. A hand poked out from beneath, which now lay limp and charred. The young woman silently mouthed 'Mom' as her eyes filled with tears. She bent down and tried to pick up a dainty necklace from the ground, still clasped shut and stained with blood. Her hands were too burned to grip it, so Claws stepped in and picked it up for her. "This was my little sister's," she sniffed. "The clasp on the chain was broken so she never took it off."

She lightly ran her fingers over the necklace in his hand and began to sob. Then she quickly looked up at Claws.

"What about my dad?'

Claws recalled the strange encounter with the old man—torn between a lie or admitting that her father was both a literal and figurative monster who had abandoned his family in their moment of greatest need.

"Your father was a hero," he solemnly replied. She had been through enough already.

The young woman continued to cry as Claws moved in to comfort her. As the guilt set in, he held her close and looked out over the burning home that surrounded them. The night seemed almost serene as he watched her world turn to ash with only the crackle of the fire and her muffled tears breaking the silence. Her father was gone, though perhaps for the best. Claws knew nothing would bring back the life this fragile beauty had lost, but if his secret could at least preserve that loving memory for a little longer, it was a burden he would gladly bear.

So, as the wood softly burned, then smoldered, then died, they stood in each other's arms. Soon her tears slowed to an emotional sniff, and she lifted her head to watch the flames as well. This moment was so perfectly horrifying in its beauty that neither dared to consider what lay beyond their embrace. For Claws, he felt drawn to this woman and stronger in her presence while she, despite all the carnage that surrounded them, had never felt so secure.

And so, they stood.

That was, until the young woman's father wandered back—no remnants of his monstrous transformation left about him, of course—as he stared at the ashen homestead in disbelief.

"Holy hell, what happened here?" he gruffly pondered, with surprisingly genuine surprise.

"Dad?" the young woman asked, staring at the man in confusion while Claws dropped his head to await the painful revelation of his lie. He knew that lying about her father's death would probably come back to haunt him eventually, but he had been almost certain it would take years, not minutes, to unravel. If ever.

"I thought you were dead. You said he was dead!" she scolded as she turned on Claws.

"Technically, I said he was a hero—you made the connection on your own. But I only said it to spare your feelings."

"Do I know you?" asked her father, who had now focused his attention on Claws, seemingly detached from the problem at hand.

Claws was offended by the father's forgetfulness. "Yes, you were fighting the dragon and I came to help. We met not 30 minutes ago."

"A dragon? Couldn't be," replied the old man, who was struggling to concentrate as bacteria silently feasted on his nervous system. He dismissed the crazy stranger's claim reflexively. "I haven't seen one of those in years."

Losing patience, Claws raised his voice. "Yeah, you might have missed it. You seemed pretty keen to get out of here and leave us to fight it!"

The father had begun sweating and his breathing was rapidly increasing. "I would never run out on my family. I love them," he growled through gritted teeth.

"Dad, are you OK?" The woman looked on with concern as she wiped the lingering salty droplets from her cheek.

Claws continued his assault. "Yeah, well, I think you love someone *else* just a little more don't you, Pops? You're a little more comfortable in saving your own skin first."

"I think I would remember a dragon if I saw one, sir, and I certainly wouldn't run from it," he was shifting his weight from side to side anxiously.

"Dad, what's going on? You know there was a dragon, look at the back of the house and you'll see it yourself," said the young woman, tears again welling in her eyes.

"Oh, so you're turning on me as well, Befana, you little wretch?" His hand had now begun twitching and his mood was darkening.

Claws stepped in to protect the doubting daughter and forcefully pushed her father back. "Hey, back off, all right! Just coz you're old, don't think that means I won't put you on your ass."

"I wouldn't doubt it, since your only life skill is how to swing a fist. I remember you now, you knock people senseless for a living in those bars. Well try living here in the real world and see how long you survive. Thug!" the man spat back.

Befana turned to Claws and gently put a hand on his chest before he could retaliate, saying: "No wait, I think something's wrong. Trust me, I know when he's angry, but this is something else." And she was right.

The human brain is a beautiful blend of very different skill sets. A ragtag crew of brain bits hired to pull off the literal heist of a lifetime as they fumble your meaty carcass through 80-odd years of adventures. There are thinking bits, breathing bits, hearing and seeing bits, creative bits and speaking bits, plus one more tiny spot at the base of the brain, the amygdala—a vestige of our primal past. The amygdala is home to that kill-or-be-killed survival instinct that still rules most of the animal kingdom, but that we have evolved to repress. So, when *it* screams "Hit him! Hit him!" to that idiot who steals our parking spot, the voice of evolution, our rational frontal lobes, step in like the young woman now pressing her hand to hold her giant protector at bay, saying, "Calm the f*** down." For her father, that voice had faded to a whisper due to the zombie disease now ravaging his system, and a more devilish impulse was screaming in his ear.

The father looked at the expired dragon and then at the incinerated house as Befana gently grabbed his hand to comfort him. But rage and confusion boiled in his blood, and her gesture proved the final tipping point.

"Don't you touch me!" he snarled. "What's going on?" he shouted as he grabbed his head and squeezed it like it was breaking apart, then began to stumble. "Arrrrrrrr!" He leaned back, convulsing and growling, his eyes filling with blood. Claws pulled the woman closer as they watched.

Suddenly the father's head snapped forward and his eyes locked onto the pair. However, they were no longer *his* eyes but that of something else, something evil. Claws took a slow step in front of Befana to shield her from the being that was once her father. To Claws' surprise, Befana then stepped back in front of *him*. The creature growled again and readied to charge but could manage just one step before the dragon sprang to life again, lunging forward and swallowed him whole. The giant reptile scratched its head like a dog chasing a flea, breaking off most of the protruding arrows before taking off and flying into the distance.

Claws and the young woman were left staring up at the sky as it disappeared over the horizon.

No sooner did it leave their view, the young woman hurriedly grabbed her bow and quiver and took Claws by the arm, her dexterity still limited by the burns.

Mortus finally arrived back from the bar dragging a large bag. "I couldn't remember what you wanted so I just brought your whole bag," he wheezed.

"Good, he's going to need it," Befana interjected.

"What are you doing?" Claws asked, hoping the answer he expected was not the one she would give.

"Come on, we're going after it," Befana said. Unfortunately Claws had guessed correctly.

Claws hesitated, looking defiantly at her. "We? Also, why?"

"Look, my family is dead, and I hold that thing responsible," Befana said. "Maybe you, as well. I haven't decided yet. But you owe me one so you're going to help me find the dragon while I make up my mind about whether I like you or not."

Claws began protesting as she dragged him along. And he wasn't 100 percent sure, but she may have just told him that she liked him. In any case, he'd be pondering that question over a few *she loves me, she loves me nots* at the first garden bed he could find.

"OK, firstly, I was fine," he whined defensively. "I didn't need any help. And secondly, I told you already, I never said your dad was dead, I just let you think it. No, wait, that sounds just as bad. Try and think of it more as a positive deception. I mean, it was the truth eventually, I just didn't think you would find out so soon. OK, now I can hear myself talking and even I don't believe it so I'm just going to stop digging. I'm going to put down the shovel and just sit in the hole and let you decide..."

The pair disappeared into the forest to the sound of his feeble protestations, with the shadowy figure of Mortus stumbling behind, struggling to carry his and Claws' bags.

As Befana led the way, her homeland soon faded from view, but the loss still weighed heavy on her heart, though for some strange reason her spirits were insurmountably high.

Maybe it was the hulking great man she held by her side with a vice-like grip or maybe it was the promise of bloody revenge with a giant prehistoric monster—whatever it was, she was excited by the adventure ahead and couldn't wait to get started. Though she may soon live to regret that decision.

Well... *if* she lived.

4

AN ODD COUPLE

The following morning, Claws awoke in their forest campsite with a delicate arm draped over his shoulder. He didn't really consider himself to be the 'little spoon' type of cuddler, but any excuse to get closer to Befana was a concession he would gladly make. He smiled as he snuggled in. It clearly hadn't taken her long to succumb to his charms. In fact, aside from nearly being eaten by a dragon, and a small rock digging into his back for most of the night, he'd had a pretty solid evening and slept like a baby.

His eyes wandered around their little haven. The term 'forest' was probably a generous descriptor since there wasn't a whole lot of tall timber available in these harsher climates. A drab collection of tall, bendy sticks was probably more accurate, but as the sun beamed down through the wispy canopy overhead and the birds began clearing their lungs, life was returning in the introductory hours of the day. There was still a glistening hint of dew on the smattering of bushes dotted around the clearing. The birds soon found their voice and were belting out their morning tune, while Befana was cooking up a few vegetables and some eggs she must have plucked from a nearby nest. *Yep, today is turning out to be a pretty good...* Claws held that thought as he considered the soft hand that had been sleepily caressing his chest, then looked back at Befana, who was crouched near the fire and returned his gaze with a smile.

"Well, hey, sleepyhead. I was wondering when you two planned on joining me," she said with a hint of mockery in her voice as she stood up and wiped her hands. "I was starting to get jealous."

Claws looked behind him to see Mortus drooling on his shoulder and realized two things: first, the small 'rock' was perhaps more organic in composition than he'd originally thought. And second, if that was the case, then perhaps Mortus had enjoyed an even better night's sleep than *he* had.

Claws reached back and peeled away the offending arm of his unlikely snuggle buddy before scooting away. Thankfully, the 'rock' he'd become all too familiar with was still concealed in his bedfellow's pants.

He wandered over to Befana's campfire.

"Tomato?" She offered a sloppy blackened blob sliding around the plate.

"Yuck," Claws could not turn his nose up any higher or faster. "I'd rather lick chocolate from the bottom of your shoe—and that's knowing full well it probably isn't going to be chocolate—than take a bite of that horrible thing."

"So that's a no," Befana said, unimpressed.

"Yes," Claws replied, now embarrassed at his outburst.

"Well, OK, so you must have a few bruises on you today. You took a beating last night," she seemed to brighten up, looking a little too happy at the thought of his injuries.

"Yeah I...," Claws began, as he felt for his ribs. Strangely, they felt fine.

"I really...," he began again, this time reaching for a shoulder he'd nearly dislocated when he was slammed into the wall, but again he rotated the blade with no hint of pain. He stared at nothing in particular for a moment as he considered the phenomenon.

"Actually, I feel fine," he surprisingly concluded.

"Wow, maybe you're tougher than I thought," Befana said. She didn't really believe him but was amused by his tough guy act.

"I *have* had this terrible heartburn for most of the night though," he whined, confirming her suspicions that he really was just a big marshmallow underneath. Soft. "Oh, ho, hooo! What about you?" Claws asked, turning his focus to the scarring on her hands after he nearly coughed up a lung.

Befana looked down and could still see the imprint of the locket burned into the skin. She flexed her hand with limited dexterity until it slowly regained some range. She, too, was opting for a tough guy approach to her injury, despite the searing pain with each minuscule flinch of her hand. "I'm fine," she lied.

Eventually Mortus rejoined the conscious realm and headed over to share a brief meal with the others so they could get out of this horrible-looking forest. "So what exactly is our plan here going forward?" he quizzed the pair, without so much as a smile or hello.

"Well," said Claws, who actually didn't know what the plan was, but really wanted to show Befana he was listening and on board with whatever she wanted him to do. Unfortunately, he hadn't been doing much of the first part, which was making it difficult to contribute. "We're going to help this beautiful woman, tooooooo." He stalled for time. In truth, he had spent more time staring at her chest like a horny teen than actually listening to her plan, so he was really just hoping the answer would randomly pop into his head if he waited long enough for the little librarian in his head to find the book marked 'Times You Should Have Been Listening' and rescue his mouth. If not, then perhaps Befana would take his juvenile ogling as a compliment to her beauty. Claws wondered how he was going to get out of this, as the vowel extended past 20 seconds, and he could feel his lungs starting to squeeze as he ran out of breath.

Befana could have rescued him. She knew he had no idea, but was enjoying watching him squirm. She could never understand the male obsession with breasts.

And people say women are the hormonal ones, she thought skeptically. *Please. A bit of skin catches their eye and the boys might as well be trying to think with a block of wood between their ears. Like there isn't enough blood in their bodies to sustain two major organs at once.*

More importantly, she was curious to see whether he would simply admit he was an idiot for not paying attention, or pass out trying to hide his juvenile obsession—which would, of course, lend more weight to the idiot theory. Finally, she took pity and jumped in to save him by finishing his sentence. "To hunt down the dragon and avenge my family," she declared.

Mortus was flat in his reply, not really known as a people person—unless of course that person was wealthy—although he had developed a higher level of tolerance for Claws, like an immunity he had spent years building up through the necessarily proximal nature of their manager-client friendship. "And how much is she paying us?" he queried.

"Mortus, don't be rude," Claws was intensely defensive, which was a surprise even to himself.

"I'm sorry," said Mortus, feigning sincerity as he turned toward Befana. "How much would you *like* to pay us?" he asked politely.

Befana was speechless for a moment before Claws interjected, "That won't be necessary, Morty. You saw what she went through. I want to help her out."

"And what about us? We have three villages booked ahead of us," Mortus exclaimed, growing frustrated by the distraction this woman was bringing to their little team. Meanwhile, Befana was keeping well out of this one to let them have their squabble.

"I'm sure there will be no shortage of people wanting to take a swing at me when we're done. Look at *your* face, it's only taken me 30 seconds and you already look like you want to hit me," Claws laughed.

Mortus was certainly bubbling up to that level as the conversation wore on. "I had to work hard to organize those fights. It took me days of travel!" he snarled. It hadn't really, of course, as he'd hired people to travel for him to make the arrangements, but he had still had to pay them, and that was worse by his standards.

"Come on, Morty," Claws wasn't taking this argument anywhere near as seriously. "You may have had some chatter to deal with but I'm the one swinging my fist. We've got plenty of gold. Let's just take this as a holiday," he suggested.

Now Mortus was a smart guy. He didn't have the brawn, like his brick-shithouse-sized associate, but his brain could kick the crap out of this idiot's meat melon any day. And what Claws said hurt; it pissed him off. His 'chatter' had as much a part to play in their success as Claws' ability to flex a bicep. Mortus wanted to hit him but what purpose would that serve?

Let off some steam? Sure, he thought.

Crack a tooth, while breaking my own wrist in the process? Probably.

Divide our friendship, or worse, ruin our business—never to work another fight again? Definitely.

No, there were smarter ways to seek revenge, so for now he would wait. His time would come. "You know you're right," he sneered apologetically. "Perhaps a little break might do us some good."

"That's the spirit," Claws smiled. "Now, come and grab some eggs. Let's try and put some meat on those bones."

Mortus grumbled all the way to his makeshift plate, which Claws had fashioned from some fallen tree bark. Morty hadn't always been this bitter. When he ran into his prize bull a decade ago in a run-down old beer hall, they had genuinely connected as friends.

On that day, Morty had just finished another long shift treating patients, and was feeling just about ready to hang himself. Now, you would think an esteemed profession in healthcare would be a more rewarding experience for a wealthy Dane such as himself, but this was a time when medicine was still largely experimental, and the climate in their little town did no favors for the practicing physician. He was actually quite a brilliant doctor, but with hunting still the big-ticket trade in the country, the freezing waters where they chased the seals often killed or crippled the hunters, leaving Morty little more to do than sign the death certificate. His success rate was not overly high, and with every spearman who plunged into the deep, so too did his approval ratings.

As he pondered the structural integrity of a beam overhead, he noticed a fellow sad sack walk in. It was Claws. "You owe me a drink Joe," sighed Claws to the barman. "Didn't even last the week at this one." He raised his cup as soon as it found his hand. "To complete and utter failure," he toasted grimly.

Morty normally wasn't one to socialize with the common folk. Quite frankly, he was disgusted by them most of the time, so he was certainly surprised to find himself wandering over for a chat. "To failure," he raised his drink to his fellow lost soul. "The first steps in every great adventure."

And in the clinking of cups, a friendship was born, as the two found solace together in the bottom of a beer mug. At least, that's where they spent most of the night looking, and boy did they look deeply into a lot of mugs.

The pair drank until the early hours of the morning, when the reality of their boring lives eventually caught up with them as Mortus readied to leave for another day of mind-numbing work. They would have parted ways there, never to speak again, if it weren't for some thug and his mates who took a shot at Mortus as he was exiting the hall.

"A pleasure to meet you stranger," Morty waved as he stood at the door. "I hope we meet again sometime." He turned to exit the bar but in his inebriated state he took a wider turning circle than usual and crashed into the arm of the burly brute. Drinks were spilled, words exchanged, and he was aggressively tossed against a wall.

Claws sprang into action. As the thug took another hefty swing at poor Morty—who was somehow still standing, but dazed, with his back against the wall—Claws punched the man in his swinging arm, connecting with the forearm, which caused the thug to miss his target and smash his fist through the timber wall a few inches to the right of Morty's head.

"Good to see you again," Morty smiled, slurring through a mix of concussion and booze. As the thug winced in pain, Claws grabbed the now undoubtedly broken hand and twisted it backward, invoking shrieks from the once-tough guy. The thug's friends stepped forward, but Claws—one hand effectively behind his back holding the screaming man hostage—used his other hand to swat their punches away before dispatching the pair with a series of kicks to their knees like an axe man felling oak trees. With their kneecaps now splintered, they dropped to the floor, and Claws spun on the spot to deliver a heavier kick to their screaming faces, forgetting he was still holding their leader's broken hand, which made some horrible grinding and cracking sounds as it twisted in his turning grasp. But there were no screams to be heard this time, just a tiny whimper before he passed out from the pain.

Claws leaned forward to help Mortus to his feet—his drinking mate now staring in awe at his hero—such power! No one had ever done anything like that for him before. He didn't know how to respond, he wanted to hug him but didn't want to seem too pathetic and grateful. Perhaps just a firm handshake, or a knowing nod. Before a decision could be made, Mortus instead, got a solid slap on the back, which felt harder than the wall he'd just peeled himself from. "You OK, little guy?" asked Claws. "You took quite a shot there. You're pretty tough," Mortus searched Claws' face for a hint of sarcasm in the compliment, but it seemed genuine.

He began to reply when suddenly a man wandered over to Claws and shook his hand. "Impressive effort, lad," he grinned. "Looks like you can handle yourself in a fight.

Listen, I'm organizing a little exhibition in a few days. What would you say to earning some gold for that kind of performance?"

Mortus' ears pricked at the sound of money. *Nothing like the smell of profit to sober a man up*, he mused as he began mulling over scenarios in his head.

"Absolutely!" Claws was all too eager to jump on board and practically leaped at the chance when the man started counting out coins. But Mortus put a steadying hand on his hero's chest to hold him back.

"May I have a moment with my associate, please?" he asked, smiling at the organizer as he guided Claws across the room. "Listen," he whispered to his new friend, seeing an opportunity to make some cash but needing to shoe-horn himself into the process somehow.

"How are you with money?" asked Mortus, trying to sound professional and confident.

"I'm OK, I guess," Claws replied, sounding far less assured.

Good, thought Mortus. "Just OK? Look, before you say yes to this guy, have you considered the average going rate for a job like this?"

"Well, no," said Claws, his voice wavering.

"Have you considered what kind of annual income you might be looking at?" Morty pressed. "Or arranging savings schemes or deductions to account for losing streaks or injuries if you decide to take this on long-term?"

"It's just one fight," said Claws, attempting to downplay Morty's growing intensity.

"Is it?" Mortus persisted. "Or could this fight, if handled properly, set you up for a long career as a very wealthy hero?" Mortus was lining up his target like a great hunter stalking its prey.

"Well, I do like the sound of that," admitted Claws, falling for Morty's shameless patter. "And I guess I don't really have anything else to do right now." Claws' ego was swelling like an anaphylactic chewing a peanut. "I don't know. It sounds really complicated now. I just wanted to have some fun and a few fights."

Bullseye, Mortus had Claws right where he wanted him. He stepped in closer, put an arm over his shoulder and leaned in with a hushed tone, saying, "Then let me handle the boring stuff. I'll be your manager, so you can have your fun in the ring. I'll earn you twice the coin and all I ask for in return is just half of what we make."

"Really?" Claws quizzed eagerly.

"Just watch me," boasted Mortus, as he turned back to the man and waved away the offer. "You'll have to do better than that my friend. Do you know who this is, what he's done?" he asked, pointing at Claws who, half convincingly, tried to look inspiring and heroic. "This man has travelled to the furthest corners of the globe, challenging himself against the wildest, toughest creatures this planet has to offer," Mortus continued. "He has ripped the hair from a lion's mane, wrestled with the great grizzlies of the American wilderness, and swum with the ancient beasts in the oceanic depths." Mortus could see the man was impressed, so for a little icing he grabbed a white fur jacket he'd spotted hanging from a chair behind him that one of the thugs had left behind. "And if you've not heard of those tales, then surely you know how he came to possess this rare polar bear skin?" Mortus asked, as he draped it over his fighter's shoulders.

The man was hooked, dangling from Morty's every word like a weary trout on a fisherman's line, just waiting to be reeled in. "How?" he begged, eyes widening.

Mortus winked at Claws and guided the fight organizer to the bar to begin negotiations. "Well, then, let me tell you the tale of the Polar Punch," Mortus began...

It seems so long ago now since those glory days, mused Mortus. They had had many adventures together, and become very wealthy since then, but now this woman threatened to rip that apart. *How could I have let this happen*? he wondered. OK, he may have gotten a little lazy lately, and taken the big guy for granted, but was this to be their end?

Mortus was snapped from his flashback by a poke in the nose and a cheeky grin from Claws. "Hey, you in there, buddy?" It was annoying, but at least he was paying him some attention. "Come on," Claws continued. "Befana says we need to move."

Mortus sneered again at the forced subjugation to this new matriarch, and wondered how long Claws was going to let his genitals make all his decisions. He was like a mindless puppy around this woman.

"Quick, let's follow her then before you squeeze out a thought of your own," Mortus chuckled sarcastically—Claws didn't get the joke. Morty's smile turned to frustration. He was surrounded by idiots, and worse yet, they were in charge. Mortus followed them anyway, probably to his death, but by now he was too heavily invested to turn back. He just hoped that when they did eventually balls-up their new plan—and this he saw more as an inevitability than a possibility—that he was not to be dragged down with their sinking ship.

5

SHE'S A CROWD

As the trio marched closer toward the edge of the forest, Claws stopped a moment to take in the scene that opened ahead of them. *Greenland is a funny place*, he thought. Nothing but icy sheets blocked up the island's central spread, but it thawed to greener pastures nearer to the coastline, like an ice-cream dropped on the ground. Well, here they were standing right on that borderline where the bitter cold snow gave in to that soft creamy green goodness. It looked so lush and bouncy he just wanted to roll over in it and take a nap. When people talked about the grass being greener on the other side, this must have been the field they were looking at. If he were a cow, he would need a fifth stomach to try and process the amount of grass he was going to eat. Hell, even now he was tempted to crouch down and have a nibble.

"Disgusting," Befana sneered, jerking Claws from thoughts that could not have been more at odds with her sentiment. He followed her gaze past a reindeer taking a whiz on an otherwise delicious patch of clover, to see a new trail of smoke worming its way up to the fluffier white ones above them. It was coming from one of two villages perched on the horizon, and it seemed as if the plus-size reptile had struck again.

Claws and Befana grabbed their things and began running toward the smoke before Mortus, shaking his head impatiently, called out to them. "You're half a day's walk away, maybe half that again if you run. You think that dragon is going to wait for you?" he asked.

Claws and Befana stopped for a moment. Mortus was right, there was no way they would catch the dragon terrorizing that village. Of course, Mortus anticipated that this news would lead the budding lovebirds to a realization that there was no way they could keep pace with a flying dragon, and give up—thus returning to the beer-brawling days that had made his pockets so heavy.

Unfortunately for Mortus, the pair took this warning as a clue, and began silently brainstorming another solution. Suddenly they both looked at each other with a glint in their eyes. "The other town," came their synchronized response. "It's got to be next! Great idea, Morty," Claws called back as they started to move out again.

The other town IS closer, Mortus conceded, so the plan did make sense *if*, of course, the dragon decided to circle back. But why would it? It was probably already well on its way to a hideout or lair somewhere. They were just going to waste another day on this pointless pursuit before eventually giving up and listening to him anyway. Claws always had to do things the hard way.

Mortus reluctantly took a step to follow when his foot bumped into a large bag. Claws must have left it behind in the excitement. "Hey, you forgot this...," Morty began, but gave up trying to reach him. Claws was already too far away.

Mortus took another long look down at the bag. He was drowning in enthusiasm for what was about to come next because if Claws did actually manage to find a dragon in this town, the wannabe hunter would find more success as a human toothpick than any form of aggressor to the giant beast if his weapons stayed here. Then what good would he be to Mortus?

With a hearty groan he heaved the bag awkwardly up onto his shoulders and began marching after them. This must have been what rock bottom felt like. No more gratuitous parties or decadent impulses as was his accustomed lifestyle in the fighting game. Just sweat and pain and hard work like a common peasant. It did not agree with him.

Morty lasted just five steps before dumping the bag back on the ground in exhaustion. He was already out of breath and not even one-hundredth of the way there. The spiralling companion again found himself staring at the bag as it lay on the grass, almost daring him to try again. Stubbornly, Mortus grabbed the strap once more, only this time he twisted it around his wrist and began dragging the onerous arsenal across the ground. "It's going to be a long day," he sighed to himself.

Meanwhile, up ahead, Claws and Befana were nearing the town when they saw a shadow flying over their heads. As their eyes followed the darkened outline of the approaching airborne menace, it swung around over a cluster of colorful timber homes, as if taking a brief tour of the town. It wasn't an overly complicated layout, designed by a typically self-serving bureaucracy. In the center of town all the 'important' people occupied the new larger halls and the old stone structures left behind by the Norse. These were safely surrounded by the identical timber boxes, housing the disposable plebs who funded their power trip. Each home had a color to identify the role of the occupant, mostly red for those who worked in trades or churches, with yellows, greens and blues dotting the streets to represent other industries or just simply when there weren't enough red kits to go around.

It was a classic layout ensuring any invading forces would destroy the low-income expendables first, giving the wealthy hogs time to fortify or escape.

Luckily for those impoverished idiots in the red houses, dragons take a non-conformist approach to the ideals of social hierarchy, which is why this one ignored all their boring abodes to find its perch at the highest point in the bell tower of another old stone church—right in the center of the 'safe zone.' *Man, these things are obsessed with churches,* Claws thought to himself.

This bright yellow dragon wasn't too big—and by that we're talking three or four times bigger than Claws—but it quickly proved more than capable of doing some damage as long waves of flame exploded from its mouth, raining down across the roof of the building.

A huge bronze bell began ringing out from the church steeple as the townsfolk went into panic. Judging by the lack of defenses seemingly at their disposal, this town had not encountered something like this before, and would be a pile of ash before sundown if they were left to their own devices.

Befana realized this wasn't her initial target—that big mother was still out there somewhere—but she was happy to put in a few practice hours with the understudy before resuming that chase. And these guys looked like they could use the help anyway.

Just then a scream rang out from the other side of the town as a second, even smaller dragon set down on another rooftop. Its bone density must have been no more than a horse's given it was barely putting a dent in the thin wooden rooftop. This green reptile put its head down a chimney and unloaded its flame like a binge-drinker chundering into a toilet bowl. The flames raced down into the house, vaporizing the occupants who barely had time to get out of their chairs.

By now Claws and Befana had halted on the outskirts of the town, trying to decide which beast to tackle first. There was a large barn crumbling to the ground in front of them, and a green dragon blowing out the windows of a small house to their right. This was a lot more than they had bargained for.

"If he stays near the tower, it's just a bunch of empty churches and halls to attack," reasoned Claws as he studied the yellow dragon. "I think we need to get that green one away from the homes." The pair nodded in agreement but before they could take a step in that direction, another house to their left suddenly exploded as a big blue dragon sprang up from within. This one was the biggest of the three, both in length and in fatty bulk. It wandered through the streets, roasting villagers and kicking down walls.

"New plan," Befana commanded, taking charge and shouting to be heard over the commotion. "You take the big guy, I'll get the green one, and we take out the yellow over lunch." Claws hesitantly looked over at the blue dragon. He didn't want anything to do with it, but was happier to be taking this one on himself rather than putting Befana any closer to harm's way than he had to. He nodded with as much fake confidence as he could muster and headed after the beast.

Befana raced off with her bow clutched in her hand, and a quiver full of arrows draped over her shoulder. Claws reached for his bag and realized he must have left it back near the campsite. There was a collection of weapons in there he was keen to try out and their absence was going to make this considerably more challenging.

From a distance he could see the blue dragon was just under half the size of these houses, which was big, but nowhere near what he had taken on just 24 hours earlier. He still wasn't sure how exactly that might help him, but at least it lightened the load on his growing anxiety. The hefty creature had just finished chowing down on a small dog and was wandering down the main street when Claws arrived on the scene. He had two ways he could approach this encounter: through stealth and tactical nous, or just barreling in headfirst and hoping for the best.

Before his brain had even a chance to devise some kind of brilliant strategy, his legs had stupidly carried him within an inch of the dragon's scaly chassis, and Claws' fists were raised and ready to strike. He never had been a man of great patience. *But, hey*, he thought, *as far as strategies go, if it ain't broke...* Unfortunately, the dragon didn't seem as on board with Claws' bold plan of attack, and with an effortless swing of its hips and a flick of its tail, it launched him across the street and through the front wall of a neighboring home.

Claws crashed and rolled to a stop next to the dining room table where a family were cowering beneath it. "Sorry, I should have knocked," he groaned, stumbling to his feet. "Hey, you guys haven't seen a dragon around here, have you? Oh, ho, hooo. I left the gate open again. You know you turn your back for a second and off they go," he panted. Suddenly the dragon smashed its head through the wall and grabbed Claws by the ankle. "Never mind, found hiiiiiiiiim," he cried as the beast ripped him out of the house and hurled him back across the street. Again, he tumbled and crashed across the ground before smashing into a wall.

As Claws sat there counting the twittering birds fluttering around his head, he could see Befana on the other side of town dancing across the rooftops disposing of her little dragon.

Befana may not have had the knockout power that Claws had in his arsenal, but she'd learned to deal with that issue all her life. Ten years of dodging the hand of a drunken father had taught her the value of being light on her feet and to always think three steps ahead. While she would never have wanted to thank him for some of the more traumatic moments of her childhood, she was certainly reaping some of the benefits now as she skipped across rooftops battling this cumbersome creature.

At first, Befana attempted a direct attack on the dragon, shooting it straight in the head as she fled, but its tough scales repelled the bulky arrowheads. Then it turned on her, shooting bursts of flame that she jumped, ducked, and weaved to avoid. Each time she landed she would launch another arrow at the beast, but again, could not find any way through its hide.

The dragon sprang forward to engage in much closer combat, whipping its tail and snapping its slavering jaws at her. This time she split her bow in two, pressing each half to her forearms and using them to deflect the attacks like bracers. Of course, the power behind the tail was more than she could handle, and she was still getting knocked around with each strike deflected.

Another technique she had learned battling old pricks stronger than her, was to use their bodyweight against them, waiting for them to strike and harnessing their force to throw them off balance.

The next time the dragon swung its tail, she ducked. As the tail flew overhead, she jumped up to grab hold and swing from it. The unexpected weight on its fast-moving limb caused it to lose balance, and she dragged it down the roof towards the edge. As Befana neared the ledge she dug her bow into the last panel of the rooftop, to halt her fall, while the dragon—still scrambling for a grip on the slippery slope—tumbled over the side. The fall was too short to make use of its wings but far enough that it crashed heavily to the ground. That was a little different to dodging a human punch and throwing the bastard down a set of stairs, but the basic principle was the same.

The fall wasn't going to kill the beast, but it would at least buy her a moment to think.

Claws, on the other hand, didn't need time to think. In fact, he did some of his best work running purely on instinct, and right now his instincts told him he was going to die. Of course, while that wasn't overly comforting to acknowledge, it certainly spurred him into action to try and shake that feeling of impending doom. But as he tried to get up from the wall, Claws felt a sharp pain rip through his side. He lifted his shirt to get a look at the problem and spotted a metal pipe sticking out through his lower abdomen. Now Claws was no doctor, but he was pretty sure that wasn't supposed to be there, so he grabbed the end and readied to rip it out.

Just the tiny vibration from his fingernails tapping the metal caused his body to tense as he nearly passed out. This was going to be tough. Claws started counting down in his head. *Ten, nine, eight...* His big plan was to try and trick himself into not noticing the pain by yanking out the pole before he reached zero. So when he got down to *four, three, two* he pulled the pole as hard as he could. Unfortunately, it was firmly wedged in the wall behind him, so instead of pulling it out, he actually pushed himself further up the pole and against the wall. Now there was more slimy red metal in front of him and 10x the pain as his innards skidded along the beam. "Yaaaaaa!" he screamed shamelessly. The pain was intense, but he was in the thick of it now. Still groaning through gritted teeth, Claws began scooting forward on his bottom, sliding his body, inch by inch, back toward the open end of the bloody pole. Each shuffle of his arse cheeks was agony, but also brought him a little closer to freedom.

He could feel himself getting feint as he neared the final few inches and with a sickening SHLUCK! he birthed himself onto the floor. As he lay in the dirt quivering like a newborn, Claws shakily ripped off a shirt sleeve and pressed the material to the wound to try and stop the flow of blood pouring from it.

Eventually, the roar of the dragon nearby wrenched him back to reality. He took the sleeve away to check on the hole, and the bleeding had stopped, at least for now. That was a lot quicker than he'd expected, but now the challenge was getting through the rest of this encounter without tearing it open again. It probably wouldn't take much.

The dragon had just finished devouring the family who had been cowering under the table, the last of their screams silenced by the final snap of its jaws. Claws cringed. He'd led the beast to those poor fools, and their blood was on him. Now he needed to do something before more people were hurt. Claws climbed to his feet kicked the pole from its anchor in the wall. He raised it above his head and shouted to gain the attention of the blue beast. As he waved his arm, pain pierced his side as the wound ripped open and bled again. He pressed the sleeve into the hole and waited for an idea to strike him before the creature did.

Only one of them responded, but unfortunately it wasn't his brain.

The dragon turned, and in five steps had already crossed the street and was bearing down on him again, with flames spewing from its gaping jaws. Claws could only react by ducking under the heat before smashing the bloodied pole into the side of the dragon's head. His movements were slow due to the screaming pain in his chest, but the shot gave him a few seconds to clear the dragon's immediate strike zone, and he stumbled away as it shook off the blow.

By the time Claws reached the street he was running as fast as his body would allow him, which he soon found was not overly quick as a glance over his shoulder noted the dragon gaining at no more than a canter. Cardio had never really been his thing, even with a fully functioning torso, so he didn't need to be a genius to see where this was heading if the footrace continued for much longer. Behind a row of houses, he could see the town's central business district, where each building was colored red to indicate some sort of shop. Luckily, the people here had scuttled away like cockroaches when the dragons lit up the town. Claws may not have had a clue how to bring down this beast just yet, but at least they could play there for a while without too much collateral damage.

Claws vaulted a nearby fence and ran down the side of the house into a backyard where a guard dog unwisely barreled into him, tripping them both over. *There's a time and a place, dog,* he thought as he tried to untangle himself from the mutt.

And now was not either.

On any other day this creature would probably have licked an intruder to death, but for some reason it chose this as its day to make a stand.

The dog only had a moment, however, to savor the sweet taste of both victory and his ankle before the dragon ploughed through the side of the building, scattering wood across the yard in an explosion of fire. A large wooden beam pinwheeled across the yard, narrowly missing the pair, and smashed a hole in the back fence through which the terrified pup was not too proud to make a speedy exit from the scene.

Once again, Claws narrowly avoided becoming the after-dinner mint to the family meal the dragon had taken to go, and he stumbled through into the business district behind the yelping mongrel. By now, the dragon had taken an interest in this chase, and instead of just eating him it took great joy in tossing Claws from side to side.

He was too tired and sore to run, and he had lost that steel pipe along with a few liters of blood long ago, so he was powerless to do anything about it. The beast simply pushed him through the wall of some workshops, and when he climbed back out of them, it tossed him into another—obliterating future livelihoods as they worked their way down an entire row of buildings. Hiding was pointless, as it would just drag him back out if he took too long to emerge. Now and then he would find something to throw at it or hit it with, but it was more for his own pride than to have any impact on the creature.

Claws' mind was racing, trying to think of a way out, but the taste of his own blood in his cheeks was lending just a little bit of panic and shock to the thought process, which wasn't helping. He just hoped Befana was faring better with *her* dragon, or had at least escaped the town, because this thing was surely going to tire of him soon and then it would be all over.

The green dragon was not subdued for long, after a quick nap it was back on its feet and scaling the walls of the house to seek revenge on the light-footed huntress. It had taken some damage from the fall but with each passing moment it looked to recover a little more. Befana didn't care, she had a plan. As the creature stuck its head up onto the roof, Befana ripped up a few loose boards and launched them at its head. Naturally they had little effect from a physical standpoint, with the creature barely even slowing pace, but it did make it angry.

With little time to waste, Befana sprinted across the roof, sliding down the slope and launching herself across a rather small gap between buildings to land on the neighbor's roof. The green beast was in hot pursuit, and it shot some more waves of flame that roasted the air around her.

With the dragon closing in, its aim was improving and some of her hair burned as it billowed behind her. Finally, the dragon sent a huge flame spreading across every inch of the rooftop, and Befana recombined the two halves of her bow and loaded an arrow as she leapt into the house's chimney to escape the flames. She then put her plan into action, jamming her feet against the sides of the chimney to slow her fall before looking up to see the beast lean its head into the top, readying to incinerate her as it had done to the prior occupants. Unfortunately for the dragon, Befana was a little more prepared, so as it opened its jaws to release the flame, she fired an arrow up into its mouth, straight through the softer tissue in the back of its throat to fatally embed itself into the creature's brain.

She let out a sigh of relief as the beast toppled from sight. Befana climbed back up the chimney to stand on the roof. She could see Claws being tossed across the courtyard of the church. Every time he tried to crawl or run away the dragon kept catching up and smashing him into a building like a cat playing with whatever native wildlife it had decided to torture. Given the shortage of felines up north, Befana had always been more of a dog person herself, and this dragon wasn't really offering any endearing qualities to win her over.

The yard was actually quite nice, with big hanging lights dotting the garden beds and a bench under a beautiful tree that now more closely resembled an ambitiously large bonfire. Pity about her boyfriend dying in the middle of it, though. Wait, did she just say what she thought she did? Boyfriend? Well, it seemed she had made up her mind about whether she liked him or not. It was perhaps a little soon, but the realization was exciting.

"Aaaargh!" came another agonizing scream from below. *Oh right, the dying boyfriend. Better deal with that issue first*, she decided.

6

NEED A LIGHT?

Claws was well and truly copping a beating, but he battled on against the big blue dragon. He refused to give in, waiting—or, at the very least, hoping—for just one chance to turn the tide. At last, after another swipe had again sent him crashing into the dirt, the monster suddenly turned away and seemed to be distracted by something on its tail. Needing no invitation, Claws made a beeline for the church, hoping to sneak inside just for a minute to recover and regroup—he wouldn't have called this running from battle but rather initiating a temporary tactical retreat.

Just as he neared the doors of a tall, winding bell tower, they were blown open in a burst of flame as the yellow dragon suddenly emerged, blocking his path. He had been wondering where that thing had ended up, but this wasn't exactly how the expression 'to die wondering' was supposed to go. Claws was thrown back by the explosion and fell on the ground, hitting his head on one of those lights that Befana had been admiring moments ago. They were hard as hell, but a sore head was the least of his worries as he was now about to be unceremoniously spit-roasted between two hungry dragons.

The yellow dragon roared again, masking a clanging, ringing noise that could be heard approaching from above and growing louder by the second. Before the beast could take a step toward its tenderized man-steak, the massive bronze bell from the tower crashed down heavily on top of it, squashing all trace of life from the now yellow and red dragon.

Claws froze for a moment as bloodstains painted him from head to toe, before he looked up to the top of the tower and saw a frayed thick rope swinging in the breeze. He then gazed across to a nearby rooftop to see Befana, still smiling with bow in hand aiming right at the rope. Wow, *déjà vu*. She held up two fingers to Claws and he knew what she meant. On one hand he hated that she was keeping score over him, but on the other, he certainly wasn't unhappy with her assist. She was like his sexy guardian angel.

Befana started making her way down to the ground as Claws looked over at the last remaining dragon, currently gnawing on an arrow sticking through a tiny gap in the scales on its tail. He climbed to his feet and lifted his shirt to see if his scuffle had reopened his earlier wound, only to find it was now just a bruise! A big bruise, no doubt, but still he'd ...healed? It was strange as hell, and something he would undoubtedly need to revisit later, but for now he would take the win because the job wasn't done. As he searched for a weapon, Claws assessed the garden light he had run into before. It was basically a meter-long pole with a chain on the end and a candle encased in a heavy metal frame attached to that. It reminded him of the bucket he had swung so effectively the night before, and he began to wonder. He plucked the pole from the ground and tested the weight in his hands. *Not bad.*

At last, Befana joined him in the courtyard after collecting as many of her arrows as she could find. Claws went to thank her for *chiming* in, but before he could unleash his bell-related pun, Befana simply kissed him on the cheek and smiled. Claws was speechless and grinned like a giddy schoolgirl as he turned to face the blue dragon, which had now turned its attention back toward the pair.

He had a weapon, a woman, a weird healing superpower, and now one dragon left between him, and a long nap filled with nightmares.

The tide *had* turned.

It was fair to say the dragon was done playing, and with a mighty roar it fired a stream of flames as it charged toward the weaponized duo. Quite unexpectedly, well for the dragon at least, instead of fleeing, this time Claws stepped forward and swung the garden light at the blue menace's head. The dragon collected a shot to the temple and stumbled for a moment as it readied to retaliate. But before it had a chance to land a blow of its own, an arrow smacked into the back of its head as Befana rolled across the courtyard and fired.

The dragon spun around to charge after the new source of the pain, but this time it was Claws to the rescue. Swinging the garden light again, he crushed the beast's tail up against the burning tree, momentarily halting its assault mid-stride both physically—since its tail was now pinned to the wood—and neurologically, via the crippling pain of its now shattered limb. With Claws still clutching the handle of his garden light, the dragon flicked its tail, with light still attached, into the fighter's stomach, sending him spiraling across the yard.

Again, the dragon sought to give chase, but before any momentum was gained, another arrow changed its course. This time the missile pierced straight through the creature's eyeball, making Befana the clear winner in the piss-off-a-giant-reptile competition. As it chased the archer into the street, Befana paused in her escape to fire off another shot, but soon realized she needed to devote all energy to the sprint to avoid being consumed.

Claws rallied and quickly climbed to his feet. Aside from a few broken ribs, his other cuts and bruises were already beginning to heal. Was he immortal now? Just then he looked up to see Befana heading straight for him with the great dragon in tow. If ever he was going to test that immortality idea, it was going to be now. He picked up another light from the garden and, as Befana dived underneath him like a baseball player sliding for home, Claws swung through over the top of her, connecting a solid shot to the jaw of the beast just as a fireball was rising in its throat.

The dragon smashed into Claws at pace, and the pair rolled across the ground before ploughing into the church wall. Slowly both returned groggily to their feet. Claws' right arm was dislocated, and his leg was most likely broken. Still, he picked up another garden light and readied to fight as he wobbled awkwardly on one leg.

As the dragon approached, Claws shook his arm, trying to wriggle it back into its socket. The great beast spluttered fire from its misshapen jaw as blood sizzled on its lips, but Claws wasn't moving. Well he couldn't move because of the broken leg, but also he wouldn't have anyway because he wasn't afraid anymore. He struck the dragon again with the new light. The shot had very little power—given Claws had just one arm left to swing the weapon and his leg offered little support—but it was enough to defuse the rising fireball. The dragon quickly fired up once more, but again it was stifled by a well-placed arrow from Befana's bow. Wielding the light, Claws blocked a swipe from the dragon's broken tail and Befana ducked and weaved to avoid its fire and bites. She had run out of arrows and once again split her bow to lash out at the beast.

Each hero took turns attacking then blocking as the beast swiveled from one to the other, and with each turn of its head the lethal pair drew closer, tightening the noose. Both took some hits but got a few good ones in of their own.

Suddenly, the dragon took a lunging bite at Befana who momentarily found her head inside its closing mouth, before throwing herself backwards to avoid the bear trap-like jaws snapping shut around her neck. As she did so Claws' right arm finally found its socket and he quickly smashed the metal light down on the creature's head. The light shattered on impact as the beast collapsed to the ground. Befana then kicked the arrow that was sticking out of its eye, pushing the pointy missile further into its head as Claws grabbed another light and climbed the dragon's back. With a groan he delivered a second heavy blow to the top of its head, at last causing the creature to slump lifelessly into the dirt, one final fiery sigh heralding its end as its eyes closed for the final time.

And so, the beast was still.

The pair collapsed on the lifeless reptilian body in exhaustion. Revenge was not so much the reward for this effort. Just that they had survived.

Mortus suddenly appeared from around the corner dripping with sweat. Had he really just caught up or had he been hiding and waiting for the fight to be over? Claws suspected the latter, but tried his best to be patient, which wasn't his strong suit.

"OK, I'm here," sighed Mortus, as he collapsed on the bag.

"Convenient timing," Claws insinuated. That still qualified as patient, right?

"What are you implying?" Mortus huffed. He really *had* only just arrived in the town, but of course Claws would never have noticed. *Not while his new squeeze is flashing some cleavage*, he sneered to himself.

"Action's over dude," Befana interjected. "You missed it... again."

Mortus began to grow irritable and marched toward the pair. "Oh, I missed it?" he shouted. "Well, maybe if you two darlings had taken a look around before skipping off hand in hand you might have noticed a bag full of weapons you left behind. I thought you might have needed them, but they were a little heavy for me to carry."

"Sorry, buddy," Claws wandered over and effortlessly lifted the bag, which only served to add insult to the injuries Morty's body had sustained in dragging that thing all the way here. "I didn't realize."

"You never do," Mortus replied flatly as he slumped against the dragon's body to sulk. This was not the hero's welcome he had expected when he arrived.

Soon the townsfolk began timidly emerging from their homes, and approaching the giant corpse—their frowns turning to smiles as they congratulated Claws and Befana. It wasn't long before everyone had converged on the courtyard, with many celebrating the victory, minus the few who wept for their loved ones that had been incinerated or devoured by the marauding dragons. The town's leader also waded through the crowd to offer his personal thanks, and promised a handsome reward for disposing of the beasts. Naturally, when Mortus heard this, his reservations about this new business venture were completely forgotten, and his emotions had healed as quickly as Claws' mysterious abdominal impalement. Mortus sprang to action to resume his role as chief negotiator, raising a hand to dismiss the man's offer. This guy was so thankful, he would pay them anything right now.

"You're going to have to do better than that. Do you know who these people are?" Morty asked as he began an all-too-familiar spiel. "These two brave hunters have travelled to the furthest reaches of these lands, hunting the unholiest of monstrosities from the skies to protect good towns like yours. They call them..." he paused as he noticed one of the dragon's claws had snapped off in Claws' back during the attack. Mortus was distracted for a second as he noticed the large scratch marks had already begun healing. He gathered his thoughts as an idea suddenly struck him, "...Mr and Mrs Claws. For each great beast they kill..." he ripped the claw from the hunter's muscled back. Claws shouted in pain, but Mortus continued as he held up the claw to the town. "...becomes just another memento of their journey, each one unique like their tales of victory."

He tossed it to the great slayer, saying, "Here's one for your collection, Mr Claws."

Claws smiled as Morty turned back to the leader. He loved these stories, but Befana was quietly losing patience. Mortus continued as he placed a hand on her shoulders. "They are a sight to behold, aren't they? The bold, agile, attractive-in-the-right-light huntress, whose skill with bow in hand rivals the thunderbolts of Thor. And this towering specimen," he moved toward Claws, who was eagerly awaiting his introduction. "Take the wisdom and strength of the Allfather, and the chiseled beauty of Balder, and you may just catch a glimpse of perfection in this man. A sight worth, perhaps..."

"Thank you for that kind introduction, Mortus," Befana cut him off as she put up a hand to block his way. She wasn't doing this for the money, so she turned to face the leader. "Your offer is generous, but we really only need enough to pay our way and possibly some fresh supplies for the journey," she conceded. "I think you have enough to worry about here, so give the rest to these great people!" The crowd erupted, cheering their new heroes. But while Claws swooned, Mortus urgently took her aside to pile on the pressure.

"Listen, as noble as your offer is, have you taken into consideration your long-term goals here?" Mortus whispered intensely. "What kind of revenue do you anticipate will be required or how much to set aside? I could be your manager here to..."

"I'm sorry," Befana cut him off again, which was really starting to bug him. "I understand you two have a relationship where you talk and he tussles, but I can handle this," she said. "I managed my family's income with Mom working her ass off to earn what Dad tried to piss away. So I know how to save and negotiate and also—just to warn you—how to see through people's bullshit too, so take your story somewhere else. You want a job? I'm sure I can find you one carrying our bags, but you aren't touching these people's money. We're not here to ruin lives, we're here to save them."

Mortus was outraged and considered venting to Claws, but it only took one look at the lovestruck super-slayer to realize his brainpower had shifted decidedly south for the foreseeable future. He sighed in defeat. He could wait.

Soon the newly crowned Mr and Mrs Claws were carried away to be celebrated into the night, and cajoled to concoct whatever unbelievable stories of heroism they could squeeze from their liquor-soaked skulls. It was a far cry from their depressing introductions just one night ago, and further still from their ultimate ambition of giant dragon stew, but who were they to let these people's night be brought down by carrying their baggage? That was Morty's job now. Each hunter indulged a well-earned night off and spared little thought for their friend, who they assumed was being equally pampered elsewhere.

In truth, Morty had ducked away to a quieter corner of town to lie down on a humble old bed by himself. He didn't really feel like celebrating. This was very out of character for him, he knew, but his bones had not worked this hard in years, and all he could think of was sleep.

It was probably only another couple of days, he dreamed, then everything would be back to normal. *Just a few more days*, he thought as he yawned and drifted off to sleep.

7

MISSION IMPOSSIBLE

U nfortunately for Morty, the trio spent years, not days, chasing the beast that had devoured Befana's family. They marched from one land to the next, killing any like it to save others the pain that Befana had endured. But they were not alone in their quest.

Claws had grown stronger since his run-in with the dragon and rumor had spread that its gas had somehow granted him immortality. You see, dragons do not die of natural causes. They seemingly age but with no ill effects to their health. Left unchecked they could live forever—fueled by their life-giving gas—and graveyards were now growing with the powdered remains of hunters hoping for a whiff to join them in eternity.

However, no one knew just how Claws had stumbled onto this fountain of youth, so people had to make up their own ways of getting the gas. Some would simply face a dragon in combat, hoping to sneak a breath before inevitably burning alive. Others tried catching the beasts unawares, like when they slept, but it seemed the gas was only released at the time of an intentional attack from some kind of secondary lung or esophageal chamber.

There were hunters who tried killing them first, but the rare few who succeeded, did so only to find the extraction impossible beyond death. Some even went as far as smoking the ashes of the dead creatures or eating them in case the gas had somehow entered their bloodstream and was stored in the meat.

Of course, there were a few hunters who did work out that water could be used to extinguish their throat furnace—not that it really takes a rocket scientist to spot that naturally occurring phenomenon. Unfortunately, those freethinking geniuses then hit problem number two—dragons drowned very easily.

So, it wasn't just a matter of tipping a bucket down their throat or everyone would have been doing it. Their lungs cannot handle any level of non-native fluid in them, as they can't filter it out. The tiniest drop throws the lungs into a fit. They spasm, choke almost instantly, and die. You needed exactly the right amount of water so that it doused the flame and saturated the very well-concealed 'fire gland', but the rest had to vaporize in the process so as not to trickle down into the lungs. Too much water—the beast drowned, and the gas died with it. Too little—and the flames just burst through and incinerated you.

Now bear in mind we're coming out of an age here where people cured headaches by drilling holes in their skull, hit hemorrhoids with hot irons, and general well-being was maintained with pig vomit enemas. People weren't all that smart, so a betting person would say that Claws' secret was safe.

The species was hunted to the brink of extinction as Befana and Claws waged their vengeful war on the winged, though to be fair, there weren't that many left to begin with when the pair first entered the fray. Dragons, unfortunately, had always borne the brunt of man's ambition to claim the throne as the world's dominant species. They were the obvious target given their size and eye-catching pyrotechnic displays. Now Greenland harboured the last vestiges of their dying dragon race.

Of course, revenge may be a sweet dish best served cold, but it has about as much nutritional value as a frozen snot cube dipped in honey. So, the pair needed to monetize this vendetta if they were going to survive. Luckily there were considerable spoils to be had in the dragon-killing business, and even on their humble takings, Claws and Befana's reputation earned them significant coin as hunters for hire.

As Morty had promised, Befana was more than capable with bow in hand and her speed was second to none—though he may have understated her beauty. Meanwhile Claws was a powerhouse wrestler with a lethal right hook, and his devastating skill with that garden light had encouraged him to adopt the double-headed flail as his weapon of choice. Couple that with the lung full of strange healing gas and the guy was a freaking super-hero!

They were the perfect team.

Over time, the pain of that first night when Befana's family was slain, would fade to an almost forgettable ache, yet each time she stared a new dragon in the eye, she felt that familiar rage rip through her veins as if its flames again burned her very soul. That rage soon turned to addiction, with each kill fueling her desire for the next, until at last, only that giant home-wrecking reptile remained unaccounted for.

And then the trail went cold.

For years they continued their search, living on the riches amassed pre-extinction, but some lucky towns had, by now, known centuries of dragonless skies and, quite frankly, wouldn't have seen or remembered what they even looked like unless they stared one in the face—and we all know how that would have ended for them.

Eventually, the money ran out and they reached one last remote town they had hoped held the key. Reportedly, the town had been haunted by a huge, mysterious, and ancient creature for as long as their histories had been written. It was the last of its kind.

This had to be it.

With many of their old crew long since disbanded, they recruited some locals to help with the hunt. Even Mortus—whose role had spiraled from the reputable heights of manager to mere baggage handler in recent years—was told to grab a weapon and get his hands dirty.

Dusting off their old routine, they would lure the dragon to some rocky terrain filled with plenty of caves to set for an ambush. Mr Claws would then head to open ground to draw the beast out of hiding, while Mrs Claws and the others took aim from the shadows with bow and spear in the caves, so as not to draw any unwanted attention.

It was a tried-and-true plan that had served them well day after day, slay after slay.

But this one would go a little differently.

It was nearing dusk as Claws looked out over the open field, searching for the perfect place to make his stand. This valley had once been home to a wild rushing river, but now—long since dried—was just a sparsely vegetated ravine that snaked its way between some lush green hills. With a grunting strain Mortus dragged a bloody sack towards him, and with a great huff he let it fall to the floor at Claws' feet.

"One sack, as requested," he sighed miserably, as he released the bag.

"Thank you, Morty, you serve me well," Claws smiled with genuine gratitude.

"You know there was once a time when we hired people to do this for us," whined Mortus. "These hands were not designed for brutish labor. They are for shaking the sweaty palms of gambling addicts as I take their gold by the bagful." It had been two decades since Mortus last held a full bag of gold and the stress of his disintegrating social status had broken him long ago. He no longer hid his indignation and openly voiced his displeasure: "Now look at me," he concluded. "I'm practically a slave!"

What further irked the aging assistant, was that while Mortus was now pushing 60 and feeling every year that piled onto his body, Claws maintained a healthy glow that would rival men 20 years his junior. That gas in his lungs must have been really cooking because he had barely aged since the dragon worked its magic.

"We've been through this, Mortus," said Claws. "I have no use for an agent anymore, but I do need someone to carry our things." He was matter of fact in his tone, but oblivious to just how deeply offended Morty was. "And, as for being a slave, I'm sure even you can agree you are handsomely rewarded for your efforts, far more than any slave," Claws smiled.

"And I'm ever so grateful, my liege," Mortus sneered sarcastically, before bowing and backing away.

Claws frowned, annoyed at the ungrateful gesture. He was being so generous in keeping his friend employed, and received nothing but contempt in return.

Claws picked his spot, threw the large sack over his shoulder and marched out into the open, casting a loving wink in the direction of his hunting wife as she set off in search of higher ground. To Morty's disgust, he watched a goofy grin sheepishly wrap its way around the hero's head as a return kiss fluttered over to rest on Claws' cheek.

"I think I'm going to vomit," Mortus muttered to himself as he set off toward the caves. *But no matter*, he thought, as a plan finished pecking its way free in his mind like a homicidal baby chicken. He retrieved a long spear he'd left propped against a wall and squeezed the grip in his hand as he watched the hunters take their positions. *One way or another this madness is ending today,* he vowed. *Because if the dragon doesn't kill these imbeciles, I will.* Though to be fair, it was the Mrs component of the pairing that he wanted out of the way. Then Claws would be easy enough to get back in line.

The rocks in the ravine were smooth underfoot having been well worn by the water, and Claws slipped around on his way to his spot. It was particularly cold this evening—not that Claws ever had any trouble with that. The fiery gas within his lungs constantly burned like his own personal fireplace smoldering in his chest. Its flames crept along his veins, weaving their warmth through every corner of his body, and lending a jolly red glow to his cheeks. He coughed as he neared his mark, sending plumes of steaming hot air skyward as his breath met the chill. "Oh, ho, hoooo," he snorted.

He had chosen a particularly open channel of the riverbed to make his stand. Giving the dragon no chance of an elevated perch, while the unstable surface would negate much of the power in its limbs.

This was the spot.

He raised an arm and looked across to the caves. He could see Morty scrambling awkwardly to get into position before the disgruntled employee raised a shiny piece of glass to signal he was set. Then from a cliff to his right the glint of another object sparkled in the sun.

Befana was ready too.

Claws dropped the sack, which crashed heavily to the ground, and pulled the carcass of a mid-sized deer out onto the rocks. Dead animals were like candy to a dragon. They couldn't resist. Not too keen on working for their meal, they loved to swoop in as soon as that stench of decay hit the air.

Scavengers.

Claws kicked the body to ensure its pungent odor would seep from the flesh. They had saved this one for quite some time just to make sure the dragon knew where they were.

Soon a light breeze rustled through the empty bag. Perhaps just a change in the wind or, more likely, the giant wings of a dragon descending upon its prey.

For a second the sky turned black as Claws watched the giant shadow pass over him. He slowly raised the flail and began to swing it around his head, gathering momentum. The oscillating turn of his weapon caused the chains and bearings to rattle together, jingling like tiny bells in the breeze. A second chain—this one around his neck and garnished with many small dragon claws—joined the symphony as bone and metal bounced and clattered. Turns out Morty had been right about collecting the claws. It was a fun hobby they had enjoyed now for years.

Claws waited for the smell to draw his prey into his sights as it always had—toward its inevitable demise. But this time the dragon was nowhere to be seen.

He waited a moment longer, still cutting the air with his spinning ball and chain but soon lowered the weapon and listened. Was the beast still searching for the bait? Had it missed the scent? Or had it smelled a more sinister aroma, a trap!

Claws ran down the riverbed a short way to locate the beast but could see no sign of it. He scanned the skies and horizon but again, nothing. His mind raced as he searched for a hole in the plan. Where did they go wrong?

Claws climbed out of the failed rocky river and began the trek back up to the caves to regroup with his team.

Despite finally reaching the more stable surface of the hard, dirt field, his pace actually slowed as he now waded through the depths of his thoughts.

Just as he neared the caves, a whoosh of air suddenly surrounded him like a tornado, and he could see the eyes of the locals peering out at something above him. Claws needed no further warning. He sprinted to his right, before diving out of the way just as the giant dragon smashed into the ground where he'd been standing, sending dust clouds pluming like a nuclear blast. Inside the cloud he could see the dragon rise up with a mighty roar, spewing flames in swirling patterns as it made its presence felt.

Claws stumbled to his feet as he fled the great beast's ambush before hearing a man scream in the distance, back in the caves. He ran up the nearest hill to see Mortus being set upon by one of the villagers. But it wasn't like someone taking a swing at a guy they don't like, or two idiots just having a scuffle. There was something feral in this assault, like a tiger pouncing on its prey. Their eyes met for a moment as Mortus silently pleaded for help, but Claws knew he was too far away to do any good.

Still, he took a step in the direction of his friend anyway, for what it was worth, before a cry from Befana halted him in his tracks.

Claws' eyes widened as he turned to see the dragon spray its flames toward the cliffs above it where Befana now wrestled with a feral villager of her own. The scorching blast crashed over the ledge like a wave breaking on the sand and Befana took cover behind a rocky outcrop, just in time to shield herself from the heat. The villager wasn't quite so lucky as it cooked where it stood before falling backwards over the cliff. Such was her way, Befana was not going to go down without a fight, but there weren't a great deal of retaliatory options at her disposal from where she sat.

As Claws prepared his rescue, he again was interrupted by the agonizing scream of Mortus in the caves, though this would ultimately be the old friend's last as Morty soon fell silent. An attacker then emerged from the cave covered in blood, with muscles tensed, face twisted into a vicious snarl, and foam now bubbling from his lips like a rabid dog.

Claws recognized the look from that fateful night when Befana's father turned, but he still didn't know what it was. On this particular page in history, the term 'zombi' was still relatively niche, currently only haunting African slaves who dreamed of rebellion—the Western world was yet to realize the true threat of a classic horror movie-style zombie plague. So current sightings like his, were merely confused with mythical tales of full moons and wolf-like transformations.

But this was no dog. This was some monstrous humanoid, and it looked terrible.

The creature stood for a moment, completely oblivious that it too was about to become lunch-meat for a
greater predator. Like a coiled viper the dragon snapped
up the villager who disappeared quickly down its gullet.
It then turned toward the next local, readying for round
two. Claws took a step closer to the terrified target before
something odd began to happen.

The man's eyes suddenly began twitching and filled
with blood as he took on a similar rabid persona to that of
his recently devoured kinsman. Then another local joined
the transformation, and more until six of these creatures
now bared their fearless bites to the dragon.

They set upon the beast with incredible speed and began
biting and scratching its every orifice. The dragon, un-
bothered by their assault was more frustrated than injured
by their efforts and struggled to remove its aggressors like
a falcon pruning for fleas.

But one creature had no interest in satisfying the dragon's hunger. It instead, had its sights fixed on the young
woman perched above with bow in hand. A watchful protector, now unsure who she should help. Befana! And she
had no idea what was coming. Or who.

8

SHOW ME THE MORTY

C laws looked back to the cave and noticed the body of Mortus was no longer an inanimate corpse but was in fact the assassin shuffling his way toward his wife.

With no time to spare, Claws started racing to her aid. He ducked under a giant swinging scaley foot, punched an approaching zombie to the ground, and slid beneath the swiping tail of the dragon. He called up to Befana, but his voice was drowned out by the epic battle raging below her. As his gaze returned to the path ahead, he saw one of the locals blocking his run. Before he could react, a blast of fire rained down and incinerated the creature.

As much as Claws did love a barbeque, he was not about to slow down, so he continued running straight through the flames and the ashen corpse, which shattered on impact. He stumbled for a moment as he slipped and tripped on the falling body parts before finding his feet again and breaking back into his run as he patted out the patchy fires erupting on his jacket.

By the time he reached the cliff, he could see Mortus had already scaled the rocky walls and was crawling toward his unsuspecting partner. Claws vaulted up there as fast as he could but was too late to stop him sinking his teeth into Befana's shoulder. She screamed in pain before Claws could toss his flail at the head of his former friend and knock him to the ground.

Mortus got up and retreated somewhat as Claws ran to his wife's side. The monstrous attacker watched Claws cautiously, preparing to defend himself should he turn his attention toward him. Morty's chest pounded with fast heavy breaths. Blood poured down his face, from a large gash, though he paid it no attention. His eyes were fixed on Claws. Befana fell to the ground, clutching her shoulder in pain as Claws consoled her.

"I'm fine, don't worry about me, I actually feel really... relaxed," she closed her eyes and collapsed. Claws checked for a pulse, but could feel it slow, then stop in her veins. His eyes welled with tears as he held her. Then sorrow turned to rage.

"Don't worry, I'll catch him, and when I'm done, he'll feel a whole lot of something. I promise," vowed Claws, who turned his gaze to the monster and readied for revenge.

As he stared at his old friend who was panting like a rabid mutt, he took comfort in seeing just how little there appeared to be left of Mortus underneath. This creature stared with pure hate in its eyes, and Claws welcomed the dissociative effect this was having on their relationship. He hated the thought of laying a hand on his former companion, but on this thing, he looked forward to dishing out some serious hurt.

The monster Morty was holding Befana's claw necklace—it must have ripped it from her neck in the struggle. It then tucked the claw chain into its pocket and puffed out its chest, ready for action. Perhaps his friend was in there, perhaps not, Claws considered. *I don't care anymore.*

"I'm getting that back," Claws sneered through gritted teeth. "And I hope I have to pry it from your cold dead fingers."

Beside the creature he noticed the tossed flail lying impotently on the ground. His task would have been made considerably easier with that in hand, but he was kind of looking forward to getting his hands dirty first anyway.

Without a second thought he charged at the monster-Mortus, surprised by how quickly it moved, something he would not have expected from his spindly former associate. With little concern, it dodged his swinging arm and threw him away, sending him crashing into a rocky wall.

It was fast.

Claws shook himself off only to be set upon by the creature again, which swung wildly like an untrained street brawler. Claws had little trouble blocking or dodging most of the shots, but each countering punch of his own barely registered a pause in its onslaught. It was like the delicate rose petal that once was Mortus, had been replaced with an invincible block of granite—or at least a creature now oblivious to the heavy damage being done to its body. In contrast, Claws was definitely feeling every shot that slipped through his defenses, and his body was more like a bag of marshmallows at this point than a block of anything.

As his pain threshold rocketed toward its peak, Claws wound up a hail Mary and slammed his fist into the creature's chest, feeling at least a portion of its rib cage crumble under his strike, but instead of recoiling in pain it just grabbed him by the throat and levered him up against the wall—rabid with adrenaline as its veins pulsated in its arm.

It was strong.

Soon his feet left the ground as monster-Morty lifted him higher before beating into his face with its free arm—swinging mercilessly at the captive prey while Claws did his best to block the free-flowing assault. He kicked the creature several times in the chest, which only angered it more as it nearly crushed his throat.

"You know I... never think... brain... stand," stammered Mortus. He shook his head for a moment, trying to gather his thoughts but it was clearly a mess up there in his head. "You... dog... kill... never weak... arrrgh!" Mortus roared with frustration at the shambolic collapse of his less than impressive expository rant.

As the grip of monster-Mortus loosened with the unexpected distraction, Claws took his chance and kicked down with all his strength on its kneecap to snap the joint from its socket. As bone now erupted through several points in the monster's leg following the sickening crack of success, the once-friendly fiend lost its balance, falling down on one broken knee. Unfortunately for Claws it still firmly gripped his throat and brought him down too.

Claws fell to the ground and stared the monstrous Morty right in the eyes, their faces just inches apart. He could smell its foul breath on his face and it, his. Suddenly its expression changed, and Claws saw pain. Then for a moment, he caught a glimpse of his old friend looking back at him as he seemingly returned to normal. The look was confused, scared—like a pure mind battling some demonic possession.

"Mortus, are you in there, buddy?" Claws wheezed with the limited oxygen he could siphon through his fast-collapsing windpipe. "This isn't you. You need to fight this."

Morty's grip began to loosen amid his confusion. Claws tried to take the opportunity to remove his hand but as soon as force was applied he saw the anger begin to resurface.

Then the evil smile returned. "Oh, it's all me," came the chilling reply. "Just... better." Morty's gloating was to be short-lived as suddenly he was overcome with pain as the broken kneecap sizzled underneath him, and he clutched his stomach—his ribcage churning like a cement mixer. Claws again took his chance to quickly grasp the offending arm that still clutched his throat, and this time was able to twist it, dislocating the joint to release the monster's grip. Mortus cried out again as Claws kicked him backwards and readied to finish him off. But Claws hesitated as he approached his target. He had dished out some serious damage to this opponent and Mortus barely flinched, but now here he was screaming in pain from a simple kick? Talk about a delayed reaction!

Suddenly another creature poleaxed Claws from his thoughts as it leaped out of nowhere and joined the fight. It tackled Claws to the ground and pinned him, while trying to bite at his throat. It must have been one of the zombie locals that had escaped the dragon.

Claws struggled with the intruding local, but like Mortus, it was just too strong in this monstrous state.

Meanwhile behind them, Mortus growled as he twisted his leg back into place—the limb grinding and clicking like a bike chain slipped from its rings. When it was done, he then clutched his head for a moment like a madman plagued by a thousand voices storming his mind.

Maybe that sickness is finally going to finish him off, thought Claws. At least that was one less problem he would have to deal with. Unfortunately, the moment didn't last, for as quickly as Mortus had collapsed, he now stopped, stood up and relaxed. Morty gazed around the battlefield, taking in the experience as if seeing it for the first time in his life. He turned to Claws and stared. As Claws returned the gaze, he could see the gash on Mortus' forehead had closed over to a deep scar. His leg, too, was a mess but looked better than it had.

"Ow, that was excruciating," the monstrous foe said, shaking his head. "Like my brain was tossed in a wine barrel and trampled to a liquid by 50-year-old women with fungal infections." He took note of Claws' bewildered expression and remembered what he was doing. "Right, sorry. There's nothing like death to make you feel so alive." Mortus looked surprisingly chipper considering what he had just gone through. "But to the situation at hand. You know I never could understand why it was so hard for you to respect me. I was so pathetic and weak while you were, well, you. But now..."

Claws continued to grapple with the zombie local but could escape neither its grip nor this monologue.

Mortus closed his eyes as he continued to speak. "My brain is reactivating at an astonishing rate. All the little wheels turning inside, and it's all beginning to make perfect sense. All these years you've tolerated my inadequate companionship out of pity, like a lame dog. We were never equals; our friendship was a convenience." Mortus nodded to the zombie local. "Well, no more."

"Mortus, I'm sorry but..." Claws' apology was cut short when suddenly the monstrous counterpart threw him toward Mortus, who greeted the fading hero with a short jab to the chin before effortlessly working him into a headlock.

"No buts. I'm making the decisions now. I'm in charge," said Mortus.

Claws struggled a little longer before finally accepting his incapacitation and sat still, though his eyes continued their frantic search for some escape. He could hear a distinct sizzle coming from Mortus' dislocated arm. Mortus heard it too and violently shook the offending limb until the elbow popped back into place with a sickening crack and the sizzling continued.

Then Claws noticed the zombie local was now clutching his double-headed flail. It swung it inquisitively, like a baby testing a new toy, and once confident in the mechanics of the device, it looked back at Claws with a sneer.

Claws was trapped.

He squirmed in vain as the creature advanced, but he had nowhere to go. The local raised the flail and readied to strike, taking one big swing and... threw it. The flail sailed past Claws' head and over the edge of the cliff.

Mortus sighed. OK, so maybe it hadn't quite worked out the mechanics of it. It just copied what Claws had done with the weapon earlier. In frustration, Mortus threw the embattled hero toward the cliff as he wandered over to deal with his imbecilic minion. Claws slid through the dirt towards the cliff edge, digging every available body part into the ground to try and slow his momentum. As his head and shoulders tipped over the ledge with his hips threatening to follow, his foot managed to snag on a jutting rock and he hung for a moment afraid to move. As he gazed down through a cloud of dust, Claws suddenly noticed the flail rising toward him, right into his hand and, for a second, he welcomed the surprise. Unfortunately, as the dust cleared a little, he could see that it was sitting on the nose of the dragon, which was scaling the wall to confront them.

As the flail lifted closer, he reached back his hands to grab the ledge and pulled himself back up. Once safely topside, he saw behind him the zombie local approaching after an aggressive shove from Mortus, and it seemed ready to prove its worth to its new master.

When the giant eyes of the dragon drew level with Claws, he wasted no time in snatching the double-headed weapon. He pressed a small lever on the staff, which opened a panel allowing the chain from the second ball to fall to the other end of the staff. He then released the lever locking the two chains in place. With a lethal ball and chain now hanging from either end of his staff he swung the weapon, forcing the creature to jump back out of the way. Claws then twisted the staff, separating his weapon into two single-headed flails, and advanced on the creature using one weapon to swipe its legs out from under it, and the other to smash down on its head when it hit the ground with crushing lethality. The pulsating veins across its now headless corpse surged with blood as its jacked-up heart continued working harder and harder to fight the body's death, until at last it exploded in a sensational spray.

Claws climbed to his feet beside the unconscious Befana, and noticed Mortus disappearing into the distance. He took a moment to recover and thought about giving chase, but he was now left to deal with a far more intimidating foe.

The dragon stared down at the hunters, and the look in its eyes said it was ready for round two. Three arrow-sized scars were carved into the side of its head, like a scorecard scratched into its skin. One final zombie was still scrambling its way up the dragon's shoulder, but it casually flicked its head to one side and swallowed the pest whole. Nothing was going to distract it from this little reunion.

Claws stood firmly in front of his wife to protect her—weapons at the ready—staring down the dragon. He looked deep into its eyes for a moment as it rose up above the cliff before realizing it wasn't returning his gaze. It was actually looking behind him, and Claws soon understood why. He began to hear the snarling anger of his freshly turned partner steadily loudening behind him.

Befana was now one of them.

Given the extreme reaction the mysterious 'disease' had brought out in Morty—amplifying the nefarious ambitions of an otherwise cowardly weakling—he shuddered to think what secrets lay beneath the surface of his sexy, now scary, hunting wife.

She stared with unwavering intensity right through Claws at her target. This disease had laid waste to a mental barrier that had formed through centuries of human evolution, one which separated our new-age intelligence and self-control from the primal savagery of early man. Her body now pulsed with vengeful rage as she embraced that win-at-all-costs, kill-or-be-killed survival instinct that lurked in the darkest parts of our souls.

Of course, there have been many people who have made a living from digging deep into that hidden rage when desperate for a taste of something extra—like a final-round boxer rising to the bell or a football star chasing the last-second Hail Mary play. Some incredible feats had been conquered by those who could master the madness within, but when a zombie got their crazy on, they overshot the mark by a few levels of gusto to embrace a darker level of adrenal insanity. And attacking a full-size dragon with nothing more than a truckload of enthusiasm certainly qualified as insane.

Befana pushed Claws aside and charged at the dragon, dodging its bite to leap onto its back. The dragon flapped its wings and took off with Claws only just managing to latch on to the end of its tail as they sailed up into the air. The woman—still with bow in hand—began stabbing at the creature with the arrows as they fought. Claws worked his way up the tail to help her, but the giant beast took a sharp turn and he almost lost his grip.

The dragon shot a jet of burning hot air across its chest, narrowly missing Befana and singeing the hairs on Claws' arm. It then shot several arching flames across its body as it death-rolled through the air trying to dislodge the nimble monster and Claws, who was forced to completely let go. After a second of free fall, he managed to grab the very tip of its wing and stared down at the imposing drop that was almost his end.

With Claws on its wing, the dragon was unable to correct its balance and suddenly fell into a spiral, crashing back down to Earth in the icy expanse of the Arctic Circle. Befana was thrown to the ground upon impact while Claws and the dragon slid much further along the ice. Tired of this battle, it continued jetting fire from its jaws as Claws jumped and rolled from side to side. He found an old sled crashed into the snow and snapped off one of the ski legs. Dodging another heat wave from the dragon, he then javelined the sled right into its eye. But the sled bounced off the eyeball, and the creature shook away the pain, giving Claws a moment to slide under it, snap the ski in half and jam it into its neck. The dragon roared but the ski was too small to be of any serious danger to it.

With its prey now cowering beneath it and out of reach, the great beast reared up, blowing more flames into the ice where its assailant had been hiding. Luckily, Claws had crawled back to huddle beneath its tail. The dragon crashed back down and began twisting and turning on the spot to expose him, but Claws did well to remain under the shelter of its torso. The dragon was slow to maneuver on land—it was built more for aerial speed and combat—which made life considerably easier for Claws to dodge its pounding feet.

Not to be outsmarted, the dragon soon realized his ploy and dropped its body to the ground, laying down on the ice. Claws was fast running out of space now and was forced to jump out into the open, but not before spotting an icy cave nearby. Sounding a hasty retreat, he dived inside the cave and began weaving through the tunnels as the dragon pursued. His first few steps were the fastest he'd ever moved as he ducked and weaved to escape its snaps and swipes, but it wasn't long before he lost it in the maze.

Exhausted, Claws paused to catch his breath—seeming to have lost it—before taking a cautious step forward to exit the cave. Suddenly from the shadows he found himself face to face with the beast once more and saw the hot glow rising in its throat. Of course, he had seen too many foolish hunters order an extra crispy I-told-you-so, to know he couldn't stick around to enjoy the aroma.

He threw himself back as a torrent of burning air engulfed the tunnel. The dragon advanced, continuing to spray flames in all directions as the scaley cat pursued its muscly mouse once more. But the heat had already begun to weaken the passage and it began to collapse. Soon icy chunks broke free from the roof and crashed down around them as Claws dodged from side to side, but the dragon was too big to avoid the debris. The chunks struck the beast all over its body, with jagged stalactites plunging through its flesh. The dragon slowed as the tunnels narrowed until at last, the roof came crashing down, crushing its body.

As it wheezed in pain it looked up at Claws helplessly for a moment, a sadness in its eyes and unmistakable fear. Claws unclenched his fists and dropped his shoulders as he wandered toward his beaten opponent. He gently lay a hand across its brow, comforting the creature with a light pat. Strangely enough, the great hunter actually felt pity for this beast, like watching a family member dying in his arms. He couldn't explain it. Not seconds ago, it was trying to slow-roast his walnuts, and now here they were with some kind of bond he had not felt since his parents found him abandoned in a pub.

He patted the creature to sleep as the weight of the icy walls soon squeezed the final breath from its chest. Its dying whimper echoed down the frozen halls before vanishing into the darkness. Then silence.

Claws sat without senses, alone in his mind—the cold numbing touch, the dark taking sight, silence starved his ears, and the only smell surviving down here was ice. It was finally over. There were no dragons left now. He had killed an entire species. A tear rolled down his cheek as he thought about the dragon beside him again. He'd killed hundreds of these things, but for some reason this one really got to him. Suddenly his mind started spinning as the weight of his actions began to press down like the roof on his friend beside him. He had just caused an extinction, but he didn't know why? To impress a girl? To prove how tough he was? He wanted to be sick.

So, this was what it felt like to be a hero. This was the revenge he'd sought after for years. He had just one sense left that worked down here, but there was no sweet taste to this victory—it was bitter and foul.

With his only exit now packed full of rubble, Claws stared into the void of his icy tomb as he rested a hand on the snout of his prize. The darkness was as silent and suffocating as his own thoughts and he resigned himself to the embrace of a deserved death. An eye for an eye.

9

WHEN I THINK ABOUT YOU, I TOUCH MY ELF

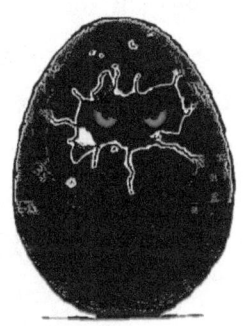

B ut slowly, as his eyes adjusted, Claws began to see a faint blue hue glowing in the icy walls of his prison. It glowed brighter the deeper it went into the cave, like a beacon of light showing him the way to redemption. Perhaps there was hope for him yet.

It had not been that long since the dragon was slain, but the heat of their battle had well and truly dissipated into the frosty walls of his prison. Yet even with a distinct chill now returning to the cave, he reached to wipe the sweat from his brow, an odd thing to be doing in subzero temperatures, but given his fiery affliction, not totally unexpected. He took a deep breath and felt the familiar burn within his lungs.

"Oh, ho, hoooo," he coughed. "Well, at least I won't freeze to death in here." He rose to his feet, still unsure of what metaphorical path his new journey should take, but for now there was a literal one he needed to navigate first, so he wandered down into the darkness.

As Claws felt along the walls, they were perfectly smooth to the touch, carved by heat rather than hand. Perhaps a dragon's doing? Soon the tunnel opened into an expansive cavern, which sparkled in the rays that filtered down through a thin layer of ice in the ceiling. Claws looked around in awe before noticing eight Labrador-sized eggs clustered in the center, with a larger, ninth egg standing on its own. As he approached carefully, he breathed out again and felt the burning sensation crackle through his chest.

"Oh, ho, hoooo," he coughed again.

As the hot air passed over the nearest egg, it suddenly began to quiver. It rocked and tipped on its side, bumping another egg which, in turn, bumped another until soon all were rocking and rolling along the ground. With nowhere to go, Claws backed up against the wall as tiny dragon snouts pushed their way through the shells, squealing, undoubtedly, for their mother. Was it the one he'd just killed?

That's why she came here, he realized. *This was her lair!* Boy, wasn't that going to be an awkward conversation to have when the kids were older?

His curiosity soon got the better of him and Claws began wandering around, inspecting the emerging offspring. They had no scales like their mother, but were furry instead, like little foals. In fact, as they fully escaped from their tiny capsules, each looked more like the winged horses of mythology than the scaly beasts he had spent his life hunting down. Their scales must come with maturity. Perhaps the gods rode baby dragons through the skies rather than that ridiculous myth of a Pegasus. It certainly made more sense.

As he stood there transfixed on the hatchlings, he had to admit it—even baby dragons were cute.

Once each was out, they just stood for a moment, filling their lungs, adjusting their eyes, and taking in the bold new world around them. Then, one by one, they noticed Claws and inquisitively flocked toward him, circling and sniffing the new member of their den. The scent of their mother, which still carried in his breath, put them instantly at ease. He crouched down to pat them—like puppies at a store—as they squeaked and chirped happily. Suddenly, the larger egg exploded in flames. Claws jumped and noticed all the little creatures surround him in a protective ring.

As he returned his gaze to the big egg, he noticed it was gone and, in its place, stood a much larger dragon than the rest. This one didn't squeak or chirp or need any time to take anything in. It was born ready to go with its body tensed and eyes fixed on the two-legged intruder. It stared menacingly across the group at Claws, watching his every move, completely still except for those unwavering eyes. As the creature breathed, tiny flames flickered from its lips as its body began the long journey toward controlling that powerful inferno within. This one was clearly the alpha, and big brother looked pissed.

Keen to diffuse the tension, Claws slowly rose to his feet and edged his way closer to the alpha male. He kept his arms in plain sight to remain as unthreatening as possible. The younger ones followed him, some pushing ahead to cuddle up to their big brother, while others remained at Claws' side. As he drew nearer, the alpha growled a fiery warning to keep him at bay. Its mane stood up like a cockatoo defensively raising its crest, only the dragon's mane was tough and wiry, it almost looked like horns or antlers. Claws dropped to his knees and lowered his head, allowing the alpha to step forward and inspect him. He wasn't keen to test the penetrative power of those weird antler horns.

The alpha took its time looking over the man, sniffing, prodding, staring until Claws raised his head to meet its gaze.

"Don't worry, I'm not here to hurt any of you," Claws whispered. "Except your mom," He reluctantly added. "I'll have to put my hand up for that one."

The dragon growled again, and its flames licked the whiskers on Claws' chin.

"OK, OK, emotions are still a little raw there," said Claws. "Understandable." He was trying to look calm, despite every nerve in his body screaming otherwise. He had many experiences with dragons over the years and none of them had been positive. But the reality was, he was trapped in a cave with nine of them, and though they were small, he had to just hope they were going to let him live long enough to manufacture some form of escape.

As Claws rambled nervously, the dragon sniffed his breath. It took a moment to process the scent, then suddenly its expression changed. Was it sick, angry, hungry? He had fooled the others but maybe this one would take offence to him wearing Mom's perfume.

He closed his eyes as it leaned in toward him. He couldn't shake the vision of his body parts flying around the cave should these little sharks start a feeding frenzy. At last, he couldn't wait anymore and opened his eyes to the warm, bumpy tongue of the alpha as it happily licked his face. Its mane had flattened back down as it began to relax. Once its welcome was complete, it casually turned away, so the others could mimic his tongue lashing until Claws was left dripping with drool.

"Well, OK then, I guess we're all friends now," said Claws, though the fun was short-lived.

Suddenly the dragons looked up in unison to see a person stumble across the thin ice above. They snarled, and each raised their manes as they readied to leap into the air and attack.

As the group took flight, Claws noticed the walls were far too high for him to scale by himself. He grabbed one of the dragons by the tail to carry him out, but it failed to rise even an inch with his weight. He then grabbed a second before a third then grabbed *him* by the shoulders, but between them they could barely lift him much higher than he could have jumped. When another latched onto his leg, they started to make some progress as he was flipped and tumbled in the air with the dragons grabbing and dropping him like a swarm of bees trying to carry a flower.

Soon Claws found himself staring down at the ground where the alpha was watching the aerial antics of his brothers. Just then it shifted its weight and dug its rear claws into the ground. It looked straight at Claws like a cat ready to pounce as its throat began to glow before it jumped straight up at him. The young dragon hurtled toward Claws and opened its mouth, with flames almost at its teeth. It ploughed into the bearded intruder hitting him hard in the guts like a bull charging a matador. He landed on its shoulders as it spewed hot flames up at the thin ice on the roof. The beast slowed drastically under the added weight of its passenger but had enough momentum to carry them up and smash through the roof.

The shattered ice caused Claws to lose his grip, and he tumbled off the back of the dragon. All he could see beneath him was the long fall to the cavern floor, and it was fast approaching as he plummeted down. The alpha landed with a thud on the ground above, its powerful legs absorbing the impact. It turned to look for its passenger only to see him disappear back down the hole. Claws cried out as he fell but suddenly stopped when something grabbed his leg. He squinted up into the light to see Befana staring down at him. She looked weak, but her grip was solid as she smiled.

"You know, I'm starting to lose track of how many you owe me now," she grinned weakly.

"I knew there was a reason I kept you around," he laughed, but he had not forgotten the monster she had all too recently become.

Befana reached down and helped Claws up to the lip of the hole. When he finally got his grip, she grabbed his back and began pulling him up but she was suddenly pushed away by a flying dragon. As Claws quickly climbed out, the dragons swooped at the woman like birds guarding a nest. She was cut and bruised by the time he got to his feet and he swatted one of the dragons to the ground.

"No," he scolded the animals, like a parent disciplining a child. "You leave her."

The dragons surrounded Befana, and her growing fear soon began to see her transform again. Claws noticed and quickly grabbed her by the shoulders, looking her in the eyes as he leaned in to speak.

"No, no, no. Come on, stay with me B. I can't do this alone."

Out of desperation he kissed her, trying to calm her down or distract her or elicit some kind of favorable result that would halt the transformation. Like the monkey at the zoo, he was just throwing shit at the wall to see what would stick. And it seemed something did.

Befana could feel his fiery breath enter her lungs, soaking into her blood, and the magical antibodies flood to her head where an army of brain-devouring bacteria had just finished consuming most of her central nervous system. She broke free of his arms and held her head, groaning as the antibodies went to work on the microscopic bad guys, destroying them and returning her slowly to human form. As her eyes cleared and her twitching relaxed, she looked at him for a moment and kissed him again.

"Thank God I found you," she sighed with relief. "What just happened?"

"You disappeared on me for a second. Are you OK?" Claws was relieved that she was back, of course, but he just couldn't shake this feeling that behind those innocent eyes of hers was an animal waiting to strike him down when he next turned his back.

"Not again," she groaned, before realizing that they were still surrounded by the young dragons. "Look out!"

Claws was baffled by the change in the dragons' aggression. "They were friendly a second ago, I don't understand!"

Suddenly one of the dragons snapped at Befana, then another. She screamed as Claws tried to shield her from them. "Get away!" he shouted.

"It's me," Befana cried. "Maybe they can sense whatever has happened to me."

"Or they're just wild animals," said Claws. "I was there when they hatched so maybe they think I'm their mother or something. You know, like ducklings."

"You ever been eaten by a duckling?" Befana screamed as she dodged another bite.

"Well, they're probably hungry. We need to find them something else to eat so they leave you alone," plotted Claws, looking around frantically only there was nothing but ice in every direction.

"And what do you suggest?" she shouted sarcastically. Claws' breath had halted her transformation for now, but the effects were beginning to wear off and she could feel her anger rising again.

Claws turned toward the dragons who were now circling the pair. He gripped his wife's hand and readied himself to attack. After all he'd been through this morning, in those caves with their mother, he felt sick at the thought of everything he had done to these poor creatures over the years, and if he could somehow find a way to save even just a few of these little guys it might start to make amends. He owed them. However, while hurting them was something he hoped to never consider, if it came down to a choice between them or Befana, he would side with her in a heartbeat.

The dragons had no interest in attacking Claws, but snapped eagerly at his panicking companion. As the circle tightened, Claws put out his arm and pointed at some of the dragons.

"Don't make me hurt you," he warned, reluctantly.

The dragons halted—listening to his instruction—but he couldn't watch them all. Each time he looked away, they continued to nip at the woman. He was losing control, and there seemed no escape. Befana began to stress and was fighting another approaching transformation.

Suddenly, a tiny shadow zipped through the crowd. It struck one of the dragons in the chest. Then another hurtled through, and another, striking the dragons and keeping them at bay. The dragons began to grow anxious and lose interest in Befana. They snapped at the shadows, like flies circling a dog's head. Befana clutched her ears. She could hear the chattering of tiny voices scurrying among them. Claws ran to her as she tried to decipher them.

"They're speaking to me," she groaned.

"Who is?" Claws asked.

"The shadows, they're talking," she shot back.

Claws looked around at the streaks of dark matter, trying to catch a glimpse of what lay within them.

Suddenly Claws was struck in the hand by a piece of what appeared to be coal. It spread a short way up his arm, forcing his hand to release Befana as it twisted and froze. The dark material then sizzled, hardened, and fell off. Another piece struck his head, and he fell back among the dragons as the black stone briefly engulfed half his face. When it crumbled away again, he gasped for breath and struggled to his feet. The dragons growled and encircled their master to defend him, swiping at the zipping shadows. Claws tried to return to his partner, but the dragons kept him 'safely' away from her. Meanwhile the dark creatures had begun dragging Befana away.

At last Claws summoned his strength and broke free of the dragons. He marched toward the swarming darkness as the 'coal' struck him all over his body and shadows zipped around him. He was slowing pace with each hit, like he was covered in concrete, and it was drying with each passing second. Eventually he fell to his knees but still wasn't ready to give up. After several more hits he caught sight of one of the shadows approaching and sprang his remaining functional hand out to grab it in the split second of opportunity. It crashed into his hand and very nearly broke free but he gripped it as tight as he dared without crushing it. He needed to see what he was up against. Claws stared into its eyes—the brightest part of the being, which was otherwise the darkest black he had ever seen. He was just about to crush the creature when the zipping shadows suddenly stopped and Befana called out to him.

"Wait, Claws!" she called. "They're just protecting me!"

"What?" Claws asked, exhausted from the battle, and finding it hard to believe he would now be denied vengeance against these violent pests.

"Apparently they think I'm one of them," Befana said, pausing and looking at the mass of darkness, deep in thought.

"One of what?" Claws was growing impatient.

"They want to know who you are, and why the flying reindeer protect you," she continued.

"Flying reindeer?" He looked around at the dragons, he supposed they did kind of resemble reindeer with their little manes poking up in the air. Then another realization struck him. "Wait, you can understand them? Well, tell them who I am."

Suddenly the one in Claws' hand broke free and dropped to the ground. It looked up at him and emitted a series of clicks.

"He says he's n-never met a human who resists their magic," Befana reported as her teeth began to chatter. "He says you're strange and he wants to s-study you."

"Yeah, well, thanks but no thanks," grumbled Claws. "We'll find our own way out of here." He grabbed Befana's hand and returned to the dragons who growled again as they drew near.

"Back off," he scolded the dragons, and given the presence of the shadowy intruders, this time they listened.

The shadow clicked once again.

"He also says y-you haven't got much of a choice," translated Befana. "The breath within you k-keeps you warm and p-protects you from their magic. But your friend's new c-condition, I think he means me," her face grew concerned. "Has numbed my s-senses, and I cannot feel the cold that is..." she paused as a damning realization lent a look of panic to her face. "...slowly shutting down my body. If they don't help me, I'll be d-dead within the hour. Worse yet, your dragons will k-kill me as soon as they leave anyway."

Claws looked at his wife—who was shivering and indeed losing color—and then at his overprotective guard dogs eyeing her off.

Befana took his hand and looked at him, stuttering through a growing series of shivers. "I know you want to p-p-protect me, and you're s-s-still my big strong hero, but I think you m-might have to l-let them have this one."

Claws paused for a moment. Of course, as soon as he looked at her, he knew what had to be done. Only his stubborn mind still wrestled for control. Not once in his life had he accepted defeat. He fought to win, or die in its pursuit, but this was no longer his fight to be won.

He eventually sighed, and approached the dark being.

"Fine, I surrender. Where do we go?"

The tiny shadows escorted the pair through the icy expanse to a waiting raft while the dragons followed cautiously behind their newly appointed master. Claws was surprised to have earned the trust of this strange fire-breathing squadron so quickly, but appreciated the back-up in case the shadows decided to turn on him again, not that he really knew who was who or had what intentions anyway. For all he was aware, the dragons could be just as likely to kill him as the shadows were. He smiled to himself. If he tried to explain to anyone else the day he was having, he would probably be committed. *Shadow tribes? Dragon pets? That's straitjacket territory right there and a one-way ticket to a comfy padded cell*, he thought.

He decided, at least for now, that ignorance was the most blissful disposition he could hope to achieve, and he would just continue following this rabbit hole to whatever wonderful end lay in store for him.

Like an army of ants maneuvering a chocolate bar, the dark creatures carried the now-unconscious body of Befana across the ice, and gently laid her in the raft. Claws hesitated at the edge of the ice. He pointed to the sky, so his dragons would keep watch overhead before joining his partner in the vessel.

After a short sail through the fog, they came to a large iceberg floating out in the water, but instead of steering around it, their shadowy captors turned the boat direct-ly into the mass of ice. Claws panicked for a moment and braced for impact but one of the strange beings sim-ply wandered to the front of the boat and placed that coal-like substance onto the ice. Within seconds it spread and crumbled away, eating a hole in the ice so the boat could pass right through the outer shell, and inside to a village which was full of these strange beings. Once inside, the shadows at the rear of the boat simply waved a hand over the ice they had just removed, and it slowly repaired itself, creeping across the gap and refreezing as if nothing had happened.

The village was a tangle of wooden huts and barns, and quite warm despite being located inside an iceberg. The elves all looked curiously at the visitors. None seemed overly surprised—like somehow, they knew they were coming—but they were still keen to inspect the guests.

Up above, the baby dragons had landed on the ice and were scratching around, searching for a way in. One of the dark elves looked over to Claws, assessing him for a moment then, without breaking his gaze, raised his hand. Suddenly two other shadows threw some coal at the icy dome, which crumbled and allowed the dragons to drop down into the village. Once inside, the ice slowly crept back across the opening to seal them all in.

As they fell, the dragons instinctively opened their wings and began hovering around the village. Some of the shadows started running in fear but soon Claws whistled to the dragons, and they landed at his feet. The dragons were still on edge, and defensively chased the shadows around like cats stalking mice. The alpha was more composed, and one look from Claws made it roar to the others. They stopped what they were doing and looked to their master. Claws lifted one of the shadows and began patting it to show the dragons they were friendly. The shadow slapped his hand away, outraged by such condescension, but Claws' message had already been received.

The dragons began to seemingly feed off Claws' emotions and act as he did, calm and relaxed. For now they stopped attacking everything, acknowledging that these ones were not an immediate threat, and cautiously exited the scene. There was a warm empty barn out the back where the dragons took refuge while Claws followed the creatures inside one of the nearby huts to help his Mrs Claws.

The dark creatures gently took Befana across to a waiting bed. Claws tried to help but Befana spoke in a daze. "Leave them, they just want to help me. Trust me, they just want to…" she begged as she slipped again to sleep.

Claws hesitated briefly, uncomfortable with this new feeling of helplessness, but gave in and sat down on a wooden chest. He rested his face in his hands and rubbed his tired eyes. He was exhausted from the day and was barely able to keep them open. Befana was being examined by teams of dark creatures amid their clicking chatter. Hot towels were laid on her, and she was fed their tonics. With his wife now seemingly safe, and his own problems in order, Claws finally settled down for a nap, sleeping right through until sunrise.

10

DEATH BECOMES HER

The next morning Claws awoke to find himself out in the barn curled up with the nine young dragons. A stabbing pain had wrenched him from his dream. He reached down beneath his back and fished around for a moment before triumphantly pulling out a sharp bone. It was probably about as long as his forearm, perhaps left behind by a sheep or pig, and was stained red with blood. He had been wondering what these creatures did for food and where they would find it. This was at least part of an answer. Looking around he noted a distinct lack of livestock at the moment, so they must have been due for a refill.

Claws then noticed the dragons lying around him and recalled the epic day he had just endured. He smiled as he looked down at their peaceful faces and patted them as they slept. Eventually he looked up to see Befana standing by the door holding a box which appeared to be filled with dog leashes.

"Our hosts said these might be useful for the dragons," she explained as she laid the box down and quietly wandered away.

Claws slowly peeled each of the infants from his body and rose to his feet. He found a fresh set of clothes hanging nearby and changed. The garments were a bit dusty and had a few holes in them, but were otherwise quite snug.

He followed Befana to the edge of the village where she had wandered ahead and stopped at the icy outer wall to watch the sun rise over the clear Arctic plain. Claws wandered over and stood behind her, putting his arms around her and kissed the back of her shoulder. As he did so, his breath hit her skin, and for a moment a wave of warmth washed over her body as her nerves were revived. She could feel his hands on her, and the comforting pressure of his embrace. She hugged him close to hold onto that feeling for she knew it would be gone soon after he let go.

"So how did you sleep?" she began nervously.

"Surprisingly well, actually," he answered. "Those little guys are pretty comfortable. How about you?"

Befana looked at the ground. "I didn't really sleep."

"Oh, how come?" he asked. "Did those little pixies keep you awake with all their hocus-pocus?" Claws was oblivious to her concern.

"Something like that," she replied with a sigh. That sigh was a big red waving flag for Claws, who had been trained to interpret this as *There absolutely is a problem.*

"Does that mean we need to go back to bed?" he smiled suggestively and kissed her again. It was meant as a joke to try and lighten the mood given everything that had happened, but of course he wouldn't say no if the option was actually there either.

"I'm still not really tired actually," she shrugged him off gently.

"Oh," he sat back, somewhat rejected but not overly surprised. "Well, you know what they say. Sleep when you're dead, I guess," he laughed awkwardly. Claws wasn't a big feelings guy and he was doing everything he could to dance around the giant elephant in the iceberg that was clearly upsetting Befana.

"Actually, that's kind of the problem," she declared.

Claws had stalled long enough. Time to step up. He turned Befana around to look her in the eyes. "OK, what's going on?"

"When that thing bit me yesterday, it changed me somehow. You saw it. I became this... monster."

Claws recalled the horrors of the prior evening. "Yeah, but they fixed you, right? That's why we came here."

"It's not something that can just be fixed," she said. "It's complicated. Since that moment I haven't been able to feel anything. No pain, no heat, no cold." She dragged her nails along the ice sending shivers down Claws' back. "Nothing. The elves said that whatever you did to me stopped it from getting any worse, but a part of me kind of died last night."

Claws was stunned by this flood of information. "Wait, elves? And you're what?" he blabbed.

"More like dark elves, tiny magic beings, neither living nor dead. Like me. They speak in a language that only the dead can understand—of one mind to another—a language they say is silent to any unevolved mind." She was referring to telepathy. "Apparently, that bite infected what they refer to as something resembling my soul, and it's sick."

"You're saying I'm unevolved?" asked Claws, sounding understandably offended and losing track of her problem.

"No, *they're* saying it, and you may not like how this next part sounds but they have agreed to teach you a language they use to communicate with...simpler beings. So you might hear them clicking from time to time," Befana simply shrugged as Claws processed the insult.

"This has to be a mistake, right? I mean, I can see you're alive," said Claws, who was really struggling with the concept. It was like trying to teach your 90-year-old grandfather how to send a text message.

"On the outside, yes," she agreed. "But this thing I've become is not entirely human anymore. My body still needs food and sleep like you, but I can't feel it. I could pass out at any moment if I get too tired. If I'm too hungry, well I think you've seen that side of me already."

If there was one thing you had to give the zombie disease credit for, it was an excellent survival mechanism. With their senses shredded, your typical zombie struggles to enjoy the basic goodies packed into the snack box of human experience—impervious to pain and occasionally the antithetical rush of endorphins that accompany pleasure, compounded by the emotional stability of a meth addict going cold turkey—and yet subconsciously, the primitive mind is always watching their back.

So, when they are threatened with physical harm, psychological strain, or the prospect of starvation—this backseat driver grabs the wheel and looks to aggressively counter the problem by pumping massive amounts of adrenaline into the system, sending them into their now well-documented rage until either they resolve the threat or die trying.

It was a lot to process, and though he still had no idea what exactly all this meant, Claws searched his mind for a response that would both express understanding of her situation and imply his continued support for her as she battled the disease. Instead, his brain met somewhere in the middle between a why and a how to produce, "Wow."

"I know," she sighed, relieved that Claws was so understanding about it all. She could always depend on him to get her through even the toughest of times. Meanwhile, Claws silently applauded himself for stumbling onto exactly what she'd needed to hear. He'd figure out all the details eventually, but that should buy him some time. Befana continued, "I should be a lot worse than you see me now. Most of the others lose more of their senses. But the disease was stopped before it had a chance to fully take mine away."

"How many more of... you?" Claws battled to formulate a question.

"A lot more than the few we ran into," she explained. "The first ones came out of Haiti apparently and the locals blamed black magic or something. They call them zombies. Now they're all over the world and growing every day. Dad must have been one of the first up north to catch the disease and now I have too."

"But you said I stopped it," said Claws, trying to follow.

"From worsening, yes, but some of the damage had already been done. You have dragon breath within you. That's why the flying reindeer..." She shook her head before correcting herself, "the dragons, I mean. Sorry it's been a long night. That's why they listen to you, and why you are the only being I seem to be able to feel. The breath gives life, it gives *you* life, and will keep your heart beating young and strong for who knows how long."

"So what can I do here? There has to be something." Claws hated this feeling of helplessness.

"I'm not sure. Death can't really be undone, I guess," sighed Befana. "The elves say they've never seen anyone survive exposure like you have, nor for this long. They ran some tests on you too while you were asleep."

Claws clutched his chest, feeling violated as she went on. "They think you have a sort of watered-down version of the dragon's breath in your body now, not quite as potent so as to cure my disease, but enough to stop it. They're still trying to understand it. This is the closest they've been able to get to a dragon or its breath so they're quite excited actually."

"Well, I'm glad I could brighten their day." He wasn't.

"Apparently, we're both unique," Befana said, ignoring his sarcasm to continue. "You're cursed to live forever, and I'll live forever cursed. What a pair huh?" Befana tried to manage a smile. She had to find something amusing in all this to stop her crying. If she *could* cry, she wasn't sure if she could even do that anymore. But Claws was too flustered to think. It was all too much for him.

"Well, if they can't fix you," said Claws, "I might as well get you out of here, and we'll figure this out ourselves."

"Look at me Claws, I can't go out like this. One bad day and I could do something horrible. I have to stay. They understand what's inside me and how to manage it. I'm safe here," she said, breathing heavily. Claws hated that uneasy feeling he now got when she got annoyed. *Women are hard enough to deal with when they got emotional*, he thought, *without adding zombie rage to her repertoire*. He wondered about sharing his suicidal observation but then realized that this was exactly why she needed to stay. It was only a matter of time before he would say something stupid or annoying to set her off and when he did, she would blame herself if she hurt anyone. She needed this sanctuary, at least for now.

"Well, then, I'm staying too. I'm sure they can make room for a couple of outcasts and their pets," he conceded.

Befana rolled her eyes at the gesture. "You're a fighter, it would kill you to be stuck here."

"Not if I'm with you," Claws vowed, instantly disappointed with himself for busting out such a sappy cliché. What had happened to him? He used to be tough.

Befana shook her head, sharing his disappointment, then flashed her "this is an instruction, not a discussion" look, and Claws knew it was only a matter of time before he caved. "You made me a promise remember?" she continued. "You're going to find the thing that did this to me, and you make him feel something. I'll still be here when you get back."

"You were supposed to be dead when I said that," Claws explained defensively. "And besides, how will I even find him? Morty would be miles away by now and might not even be as obvious to spot."

"The dragons!" Befana exclaimed, unloading the second barrel of her argument. "What if I was right last night? What if this disease gives off some kind of scent that they were tracking? The mother dragon went for those villagers, and its babies came after me. We always thought they were scavengers, hunting dead scraps for an easy meal but what if it's more than that? What if it's death itself they are hunting? The elves say nature is always seeking balance. What if the dragons are the natural predators of these things? They *give* life while these monsters *take* it. We've killed so many dragons now that we've tipped the scales against them."

"You want me to help the dragons?" Claws asked, puzzled.

"No, train them and take them with you," she replied. "They can help you find Mortus and the rest of the zombies. If they are too far gone you kill them. I expect the same for myself if it comes to it."

"So, you want me to *tame* a dragon? That's much easier," his eyes were rolling like a hamster wheel. "I wouldn't even know where to start."

Suddenly the stronger of the young dragons nuzzled against Claws' arm. Every time it breathed, tiny flames escaped its mouth as it was yet to learn how to control them. It growled at Befana, but Claws quickly tapped it on the nose. "No!"

"I don't think you'll have to tame them," she smiled at the dragon despite it not reciprocating. "I like that one. I know he'll keep you safe."

Claws looked down at the dragon and patted its head, still pondering the suggestion.

"I suppose those flames would come in handy in getting us through the dark," he mused as he dropped to his knees and looked into its eyes.

"What do you say, little guy? Won't you guide my sled tonight?"

"Rudolph," Befana chipped in.

"What?" frowned Claws.

"His name," her tone assumed, rather than encouraged, compliance.

"Whoa! When did we start doing names?" Claws huffed.

"I was thinking about it this morning," she smiled. "I think it suits him. Why?"

"You want me to strike fear into the hearts of my enemy with a lead runner named Rudolph? Why not just call him Prancer then? Or Cupid and be done with it. They're cute," said Claws, shaking his head incredulously.

"Oh, I love those names! Which one is Prancer?" she giggled.

Claws sighed as Befana's thumbprint embedded itself into his forehead. "What about something with at least a little more edge, like Ralph?" He was nearly at the point of begging already.

"Fine, you can name him Ralph, I'll name the rest," Befana graciously offered with a smile. Claws thought to argue further but he hadn't seen her this happy in quite a while, and considering the circumstances, he welcomed any distraction to bring her some comfort.

"You have yourself a deal, little lady," he laughed, before patting the dragon on the behind to get it moving. "Come on, Ralph, we've got work to do."

11

HOW NOT TO TRAIN YOUR DRAGON

C laws looked out over the icy field where the nine dragons wandered aimlessly about, sniffing and scratching at whatever scraps they could find. They were always eating. Perhaps because the growth rate in the dragons, at least in these early weeks, was extraordinary, as they were already nearing the size of a pony.

"OK," he thought, trying to muster some level of enthusiasm for the impossible task ahead of him. "Training, day one."

Claws ambled over to a rickety dog sled resting unevenly on an otherwise smooth patch of ice. The sled was an ugly mix of various colors and timbers—mostly shades of reds and black. Jagged screws poked their heads out from poles here and there, many corners were tied together with tattered pieces of rope, and the actual skis beneath it sat at slightly odd angles from one another so that it rocked unsteadily between a few small contact points where the ends dug into the ground.

A handyman he was not, Claws conceded, yet he had to admire his work. In just two weeks and a handful of tantrums, he had managed to cobble together this monstrosity from a pile of old wrecked sleds he'd found in the back of the barn. The sleds looked like they had taken some serious damage before they were tossed, which didn't bode well for whoever was riding them at the time. Obviously, Claws had been rescued himself—not too long ago—by the dark elves, and these sleds suggested he wasn't their first stranded civilian. It was a tough place to survive out here at the best of times, so he wasn't surprised others had ended up here as well.

Claws was curious to know more about their elven adventures, so one day he even went so far as to ask one of the dark elves if they had rescued other strangers out there on the ice before him. The elf didn't quite understand him at first until he clarified, "You know, have you brought other people like me into the town?" At that, the creature got very excited and pointed to the barn where Claws had slept. It must have been their recovery center.

Of course, that raised further questions, like why there had never been any stories from people who had visited this place, and why those visitors had not repaired and taken the sleds with them when they left?

With some interpretation from Befana, Claws then regretfully put these questions to one of the elves who seemed at a loss to understand him.

"Leave? Why would they leave?" the little creature queried.

As Claws glanced back at those blood-red stains on his dog sled, it then began to dawn on him that there may be a darker side—if possible—to these seemingly innocent beings. He remembered all the human clothes he'd seen in the barn; the box of dog leashes left behind; and the discarded pile of smashed sleds. And that bloody bone. He looked down at the jacket he was wearing, which had the name 'Jim' embroidered on the front. As he checked the pockets, he noted more of that dust he'd brushed off before, though looking closer it seemed dark and chalky, like the stuff the dark elves had attacked him in their first encounter. He considered, for a moment, just what (or whose) limb exactly he'd been holding that morning after.

He may have had a magical fire burning in his lungs but even that thought gave him the chills. Lucky, they called him the interesting one.

So with that knowledge now buried somewhere in a pile of mental boxes labelled DENIAL, Claws turned to start getting the dragons into their harnesses and ready for practice, when he almost stepped on one of the dark elves. He jumped at first, still not totally sure whether the creature would respond by ringing the dinner bell or sparing him for later. The figure stood little more than ankle height. To the untrained eye you would swear it was just the shadow from a hole in the ground. He didn't know if this was the same one that he had captured and surrendered to just a few nights ago. All these little dark creatures looked the same. Suddenly, he smiled sheepishly to himself. He sounded just like his old man, complaining about anyone born outside his population 200 town with a darker shade of skin than his albino-esque complexion. Stubborn old racist.

Well, not Claws. Now with the benefit of his father's mistakes, he was determined not to repeat them.

He crouched down and had a closer look at the elf. It was a lighter shade than all the others he had seen. More of a dark grey than jet black. Did that make it older? Younger? Did that tell him the gender? He had no idea. "What's your name?" he asked, thinking he'd start simple.

It clicked incoherently in response, and Claws just stared at it for a moment with a stupid look of confusion on his face. Of course, he had no idea what it was saying and really, what other outcome had he expected? He wasn't even sure the little mothball could understand *him*. Without his translator present he may as well have been talking to Ralph. Still, he listened patiently, hoping for some kind of savant-like light-bulb moment where he suddenly just cracked the code on this ancient language and could chat with it.

But no such luck.

The elf eventually must have realized Claws wasn't following their conversation and began clicking again. Louder and more expressive this time. *Wait a second*, Claws thought as he studied the creature. He could have sworn the elf was doing that thing people do when someone doesn't speak their language. You know, repeating the exact same sentence just louder and slower, because that must have been the reason they didn't understand you the first time. Well, he was not about to be treated like a tourist.

Finally, the creature gave up, and they enjoyed an awkward moment of silence before Claws broke the tension.

"I know, I'll name you Larry," he smiled. *Progress.*

The elf dropped what appeared to be its shoulders and exhaled. The argument just wasn't worth it. His true name was far more complex than this simple creature could ever comprehend anyway, plus it would probably be dead in a few days if this conversation was to be any measure of its intellect. He wasn't sure what the flying reindeer saw in this new pet or how they planned to train it, but it was certainly going to be amusing watching them try. *So just let it call you 'Larry' if it makes it feel any better*, the elf mused, *and maybe it will leave you alone.*

Larry nodded in acceptance and stood aside for Claws to pass. Claws, meanwhile was quite pleased with himself and grinned from ear to ear. Looks like he didn't need Befana babysitting him all the time. He just connected with this creature like two intelligent beings and found an unspoken understanding that may well have bonded them for life.

He wandered over to the dragons with renewed confidence. "OK, gang, can I get everyone over here so I can hook you up?' Claws was surprised when none of the creatures responded to him. He really thought it was going to be that easy. He then noticed one dragon nearby had a collar around its neck. Actually, all of them did. He stepped up to the nearest one and inspected it. He winced as he read the first name. Somewhere in their conversation yesterday he had apparently given Befana sole naming rights to all the dragons, and each one wore a slightly faded—and occasionally bloodstained—collar with an engraved metal plate sewn onto it.

"OK, Blitzen," he sighed. "Time to get you hooked up to the sled." He guided the dragon over and worked his way through the twists of the harness to lock it onto the sled. With the first one down, he then set about tracking down the next one. As he turned his back and wandered over to the next dragon, he heard the scraping sound of the sled sliding across the ice behind him. Looking back, Claws noticed Blitzen meandering along dragging the mangled wooden deathtrap behind it. Claws left the second dragon and jogged back towards the sled, but when he arrived, the other dragon had wandered further away than before.

Like repellent magnets, the sled and dragon No.2 seemed hell-bent on maintaining as big a distance between them as possible, but after what seemed like an age, he had inched them closer and closer together until they were as one.

The sweat was dripping from him now as Claws searched for the third dragon for his sled. Once he found it, of course, the two-dragon-powered sled had travelled even further in the opposite direction. Were they messing with him on purpose? He couldn't believe how long this was taking. At this rate by the time he got them all connected it would be time to let them off and go to bed.

Claws looked over to see Larry just shaking his head and Ralph watching on with curiosity. "Feel free to lend a hand anytime now," he snapped.

Suddenly Ralph yawned and wandered over to stand by the lead harness. Ralph was different to the other dragons. He was smarter, or at least more manageable.

He waited patiently as Claws jogged over and hooked him up. He smiled when he noticed that the collar read *Rudolph*. "That stubborn bitch," he grinned. Once connected, Ralph stood firmly in place and growled at the others if they tried to move the sled.

Maybe Befana is right, he thought. *Maybe all dragons aren't so bad. I could just pull this off.*

With Ralph anchoring the sled, Claws made light work of getting the remaining dragons connected, then he stood astride the sled triumphantly. "Larry, do you want to hop on?" he called to the little grey shadow. Now he had never heard one of these things laugh before but was almost certain that the sound it made in response was its equivalent. Larry just perched himself on a nearby rock to observe.

"Chicken!" Claws taunted. "Fine, I'll do it without you. Yar!" he said as he whipped the reins to snap the dragons into action. Unfortunately, Ralph didn't take too kindly to this show of force so—with a quick flick of his lizard-like head—he bit down on the reins and ripped them from the driver's hands. What the young reptile didn't know (or probably care about) was that Claws had wrapped them tightly around his palms for grip, so Ralph's outburst actually wrenched him from his seat and sent him flying through the air. No sooner did Claws hit the ground, he felt a wave of heat as Ralph incinerated the reins for good measure. As the flames rushed up the leather straps towards his hands, Claws quickly untangled himself and tossed the burning remnants to the ground. He took a moment to wipe the ash from his hands and let his brain catch up to what had just occurred.

"Right, no whips then," he conceded. "Good talk."

Claws wandered back to the sled and climbed in. He knew reins were out of the question, so he searched for another way to gain some kind of control over the sled. Alas there was nothing, so he turned to face the dragons with considerably less enthusiasm than before.

"So, how about I just say 'Go'?" he asked, but there was no response from his dragon team. "Um, jump! Run! Tally ho! Giddy-up!" he proclaimed with diminishing enthusiasm, but his team just stood in the snow looking around with complete disinterest. He knew these beasts were intelligent, but how was he going to get them to work with him. He threw his hands in the air with frustration. "Come on, Ralph," he begged. These things didn't need cute names and encouragement, they just needed a good kick up the butt...

Suddenly a piece of coal crashed into Ralph's behind, and the startled young dragon jumped, pulling the others into action. With Claws' hands still in the air, the unexpected motion sent him tumbling backwards, and he almost fell off the back of his sled. As the team bounced along, he slowly struggled back to his feet and looked over to see Larry sitting innocently on the hill. He wasn't quite sure whether to be angry or appreciative of the creature's unorthodox motivational approach, but it had certainly worked.

It was tough going at first as the team searched for their rhythm. They continually bumped and tripped as each looked to move in different directions and at different speeds. With no reins for control, Claws was really just along for the ride and was helplessly tossed about on the sled.

"Come on, Ralph, get them in line," he begged, after nearly knocking himself unconscious on his own knee. Ralph barked to the others, but it did little to straighten their line. They were still very largely out of control. Claws looked over at Larry on the hill. Did he even realize what they were trying to do? *What a funny little creature*, Claws thought to himself before he was suddenly thrown from the sled.

Meanwhile, Larry looked on from his stable perch as the rickety sled ran in circles through the now blizzarding snow. Every so often they would barrel over a small hill or rock, which the dragons had no problem jumping over, but this nearly always saw the human catapulted off the back as the sled dug in or skipped over it. *What a funny creature*, Larry thought. However, to its credit, each time the gangly man fell, he would pick himself up, jog back over to the sled and pat each of the dragons on the head before trying again.

Larry smiled as he watched the performance, not just because it was entertaining to observe the clumsy creature stumbling through the snow, but also because he was beginning to see a greater strength to a species he had often disregarded as no more than an appetizer. The flying reindeer friend was stupid, sure, but also patient, persistent and it learned from its many mistakes. *It may never be as smart as an elf, of course,* he concluded. *But these are the fundamental qualities behind evolution. Perhaps, in time, he could be trained.*

Larry watched their uncoordinated dance continue over the next few days as the team practiced being terrible. This pack of fire-breathers and their awkward pet were improving slowly on their own, but if they were going to go hunting the undead and survive, they were going to need help. And he knew there was only one species smart enough to help them. *They need elves!*

A few nights later, Claws finished packing the last of his gear onto the sled with the nine dragons waiting patiently in their harnesses like a team of oversized sled dogs ready to run. Ralph stood patiently at the front, his flaming breath flickering brightly in the dreary blizzard that had settled in. They were standing on the mainland with the village drifting in the distance, its hazy lights just seeping through the icy walls. Befana wandered over to kiss her champion goodbye with three of the dark elves following closely behind. She leaned in and kissed Claws, the life-giving pulse of his breath adding a lasting passion to the farewell that she almost couldn't let go.

"You be careful out there, come back to me safe," she cooed.

She pulled shut his large polar bear-skin jacket to keep her husband warm and patted his chest as he turned to leave.

"I will, oh, ho, hooooo," he coughed as he wandered over toward the sled but paused when he noticed Larry and two other dark elves waiting on it.

"Oh hello Larry," he skeptically greeted them. "Who are your friends?"

Each of the new elves began clicking excitedly but Claws impatiently cut them off since he still couldn't understand their language. "Yeah, I don't know why I keep doing that. From now on I'll call you Peter and you Shirly." Peter had a small hole in his leg, which didn't seem to bother him, and it just looked like a birthmark. Claws had considered the name Spot but felt it was important to make the elves feel more intelligent and avoid the condescension of a stereotypical 'pet name'. So, Peter it was.

Shirly had a kind of swirly pattern to her body, and the name just sounded pretty.

Befana tried to interject. "They already have names if you want to know." Suddenly she stopped and looked at Larry who had silently told her Claws was too stupid to understand. "Never mind, they insisted on going with you," she conceded.

Claws was quite chuffed at the support. "Well, I see I've put your fears of flying with us at bay. Welcome aboard!" He beamed.

"Actually, they said they are only going because you'll probably die without them, and there's still a lot they need to learn about your abilities," said Befana as she shrugged and smiled at him. "I think that's as close as you're going to get to them liking you."

"Well, that's comforting," he mumbled.

With that, Claws stepped onto the back of the sled and gripped the reins. Reins which didn't actually connect to—or offer any control over—the dragons so as not to further agitate young Ralph. Claws was NOT making that mistake again. These were actually just some belts he had nailed to the sled purely to give him something to hold onto for the trip. "I'll be back soon, my dear," he bellowed. "OK, Ralph." Befana raised an eyebrow, but Claws shot back an innocent grin. "We've got a lot of ground to cover tonight, so let's get started."

Claws lightly whipped the reins despite Ralph doing all of the work to get the others going. Though they had certainly grown, they were still too small yet to fly with all the added weight, but they certainly weren't lacking in pace across the ground either. They bumped into one another for a short while as had been their norm, but with the long ride ahead they had plenty of time to adjust their lines.

This time, Larry hopped up off the sled and wandered across the bouncing harnesses until he reached Ralph at the front. He jumped up on the dragon's head as it glanced irritably at the unwanted passenger. Then Larry whispered something in his ear causing Ralph to instantly quicken his pace. Claws' smile turned to growing concern as the village shot from sight in a flash as the other dragons followed the lead of their brother.

"OK, boys, easy does it. It's a bit rocky up ahead so not too fast," he begged. But it was too late for that, they were motoring now.

Naturally the dragons got faster and faster with each step as Claws gripped the sled tighter and tighter.

"Slow it down a little, guys. If you go any faster and you're going to take offffffffff!" he yelled as suddenly Ralph jumped into the air and spread his wings. The others watched, but through lack of strength or confidence they failed to follow, and after a moment he crashed back to the ground. Ralph kept his footing and pulled harder as he ran, looking back over his shoulder to the rest of the siblings and barked, as if sending an order.

Ralph took off again, spreading his wings as the ropes creaked with the strain.

Claws could see what he was doing and was a little terrified at the direction this was heading. "OK, now Ralph.

There's no need to go showing off to your brothers there. We don't want them getting ideas."

Just then the next four smaller dragons started hopping and getting airborne.

Claws called to his leaders with a tone of concern. "Now Dasher, now Dancer, Prancer, Vixen! Oh God, why did I let her choose all the names?" He had little time to lament the mistake before the remaining dragons followed suit and the sled lifted up into the air. Claws was terrified and clutched the sled as it flipped upside down, rolling and tumbling in the air. His supplies began falling from the sled and disappeared into the icy wastes below.

"Whoooooooa, stop, take it down!" he pleaded. "We didn't practice this! You're not supposed to be able to lift a sled!" The dark elves had made their way onto the harness to enjoy a much smoother ride, and clicked to one another as they looked down on the dangling stranger.

Claws, though totally clueless as to what exactly they were saying, could sense the condescension in their tone and yelled up to them in frustration. "Oh shut it, guys, all right? Like you could have seen this coming!"

The dragons continued to fly through the night as Claws grappled with the sled, finally managing to tie some belts around himself and secure them enough so as to not fall off, but by no means was he travelling first class. It was a level of comfort akin to putting the saddle on the underside of a horse and spending a long gallop being slapped in the face by its sex pistol. *Still*, he thought to himself, *it could be worse*. But he struggled to think of many ways it actually could have been.

12

NIGHTMARE ON ELF STREET

A small town lay silent as this little patch of Earth slept soundly. Soon the soft jingle of sleigh bells could be heard echoing over the horizon as nine dragons and their master cut through the skies. There was an elegance to the flight of the fire-breathers, the slow, billowing strokes of their wings cupped the air, as if they were swimming through the clouds. For Claws however, his entrance was far less graceful as he flapped behind the sled like a piece of toilet paper stuck to the back of a motorcycle. His claw-chain and weapon rattled wildly in the breeze as he gave every effort to simply hang on.

The dragons raised their manes as they approached their destination, and swooped in to land on the quiet, icy street, each one gently touching down with barely a sound. Behind them, showing considerably less stealth, came the muffled screams of panic as Claws and the sled smashed heavily into the ground. The sled exploded into a hundred pieces, sending its passenger sliding across the slippery surface into a bush—swearing all the way. As he dragged himself to his feet, he looked up to see the dragons waiting patiently at a house.

"OK, that went well," he muttered, brushing off the ice. He looked back at the sled which was completely destroyed. "Right, let's get everyone out of sight please, before a local has a stroke. And Larry, can you do something with this please?" he pointed to their obliterated transportation. "I can't help but feel it's somehow your fault." Larry clicked in response and motioned to the other elves to start cleaning up the wreck before following the hero in training.

Claws walked over to the house where the dragons were waiting, unhooked Ralph from the lead and paused to look at the door while the rest of the dragons wandered around the back. Larry hopped up on his shoulder and Ralph moved in next to him. "So, this is the place, huh?' Claws mused. "One of those... things is in there?"

As expected, he received no confirmation from his companions. He looked with concern at the house and racked his brain for a plan.

"So should I knock?" he asked, then put on a brave voice as he ran through the scenario. "Excuse me, ma'am, but I think your husband may be some kind of monster. Would you mind terribly if I check?"

He then began to wonder how exactly he *would* check. It wasn't as easy as taking a peek at its undercarriage and shouting "It's a boy!" No, this anatomical distinction was going to be harder to spot than the 'waitress' he had very nearly clashed swords with one drunken evening after a fight. As pretty as she was, let's just say squirrels weren't the only things stashing nuts that winter, and Aaron sounds an awful lot like Sharon when noisy bars mix with alcohol.

Claws shook his head as he approached the door—some things he saw that night could not be unseen. He only hoped tonight would not add to the vault of memories long-wished forgotten. But he had fought dragons and a few zombies already and he always seemed to come out on top. He was confident he could handle whatever was behind these doors.

In fact, he concluded, the key here *was* confidence. Even if he didn't believe it himself, he needed those monsters in there to be terrified so he could pick them off in their panic. He'd kick open the door to see a few zombies staring at him in amazement then blow their minds with something quippy like, "Looks like someone's been naughty this year," and then shit would go off!

"OK, Larry, here goes nothing."

He raised a foot ready to strike when there came a sudden scream from inside the house. Without thinking, Claws kicked open the door and burst in. A man growled in the other room as a young girl screamed again. Claws ran through the house pulling his flail from its sheath and entered the room with it ready to swing. "Looks like..." he began his threatening new catchphrase, but something was wrong. He stopped when he saw a hulking, strong older brother wrestling playfully with his 14-year-old little sister, and was lost for ideas. Behind them, their father sat with his back to them at a workbench cluttered with toys as he whittled away at a small snowman doll. The siblings looked up at Claws and froze, not knowing how to react.

"...I have no idea what I'm doing," he mumbled nervously to finish his sentence. Claws quickly hid the flail behind his back as he feebly searched for an excuse. His entrance was ruined, his confidence shot. "I'm terribly sorry," he stammered. "I must be in the wrong house, I thought you were..."

He was interrupted by a scream to his right as an older woman, their mother, entered the kitchen and saw him. He resumed his apology—this time to her—when suddenly the woman's eyes filled with blood, and she convulsed and tensed as his own wife had done before turning into a zombie. Claws looked back to warn the children, but they returned his gaze with the same soulless aggression of their mother, as they too transformed.

"Oh, I'm definitely in the wrong house," he groaned.

Suddenly the wife charged at him, and he swung the flail which smashed into her head, sending her crashing to the ground. The brother and sister had also advanced, and Claws kicked the sister away before the brother launched himself at the intruder. Larry took this opportunity to hop onto the counter as the combatants crashed to the floor. The heavy impact saw Claws' weapon slide from his grasp and clatter to the floor as the brother bore down on him, trying to bite his throat. Claws punched him in the face, and the force of the blow disoriented his assailant just long enough for him to roll away.

Claws sat up and began mulling over quick killing options to dispatch the brother, but no sooner did he choose an attack did the sister vault the bench to stand between them. She now inadvertently shielded her brother, ready for round two. Claws was crouched on the ground when she launched the first kick, and he quickly pulled out a drawer of utensils to block the shot. The hinges bent on impact, but it held firm to do the job. For each kick that followed, he pulled out more drawers that bent and groaned as they shielded the stunned hero, until all were hanging out at various angles from the bench. In her rage, the sister smashed her fists down on the top drawer and obliterated the entire column right down to the ground so she could continue her assault. She was strong.

Claws then scooted back and opened a few cupboard doors as the sister continued to swing her limbs, but they did little to block her attacks, each one shattering like glass. As the last door broke down, Claws spotted the handle of a frypan overhanging the bench and grabbed it. When next the girl struck out with her foot, Claws batted it away with the pan, and while she stumbled to regain her balance, Claws rose to his feet and followed up with a swift whack to the jaw that knocked her out cold.

With the sister dispatched, the brother grabbed Claws from behind. Claws looked over to Larry who sat comfortably as if watching a play. "Anytime you want to jump in here, buddy," he groaned as the lad raised him into the air. "Don't let me stop youuuuuuuu," he yelled—his final word uttered as the brother tossed him effortlessly across the room. Claws crashed through the family table, which splintered on impact. He had little time to recover before he was smashed over the head with a chair as the brother caught up to him. The intruder was stunned for a moment but was immediately wrenched back to reality by the powerful sibling's right hand wrapping itself around his throat. The room was a blur as Claws tried to gather his thoughts, but there was little he could do to stop the onslaught. As the brother began to push, Claws was forced backward, crashing into the father's desk, knocking toys everywhere. Claws was now back-to-back with the father and pleaded for his help. "Hey buddy, I don't wanna tell you how to parent your kids, but you might need to tighten the reins a little," he choked. Claws placed a hand on the man's shoulder but was met by another ghoulish glare as the father now turned to attack him.

Claws sighed with frustration but the father was going nowhere. The added force of the brother pushing Claws backward kept the old man trapped sitting at his desk. The father thrashed helplessly but he was, for now, contained; however, that meant Claws could not lean forward to attack the brother without risking releasing his dad.

In his daze between hits, Claws noticed one of the table legs was still standing behind the brother, and had been snapped into a jagged spike at the top by his unceremonious crash landing. Slowly Claws managed to lever his leg between himself and the brother, then kicked the attacker backward. Claws quickly pushed away from the chair and dived toward the brother, back slamming him onto the leg. He then stood up and called over to the elven spectator still perched on the bench, as he readied to finish the job. "Thanks Larry," he panted sarcastically before a knife whizzed by his head. The mother, with her head semi-imploded, had begun tossing utensils at him from the kitchen. He dodged the first couple, but as he went to take a step in her direction, he felt the daughter bite down on his leg. As she did so, a sharp burn seeped out of the wound and rotted away at her mouth as if she had punctured a bucket of acid. She recoiled in shock as Claws checked his leg. He was bleeding badly from the wound, but she had come off far worse.

Without a moment's rest, the father then grabbed Claws from behind only to receive an elbow to the face for his troubles as he spun to face him. The father stumbled back against the desk but before Claws could press further, he was interrupted by a spoon hitting him in the back of the head—the mother must have been nearing the bottom of her cutlery drawer. He turned his head to look back at her before feeling the annoying tap of a small wooden snow-man on his head, which the father had swiped from his desk and begun beating Claws with it. The object was far from a lethal weapon of choice but what concerned him more was the well-stocked block of knives waiting near the mother for when she finished cleaning out the drawer.

With Claws distracted, the father regained his grip around the hero, only this time he was able to catch both Claws' arms and pin them by his side with a powerful squeeze. Claws struggled to remove the unwanted pest, and managed to spin once again to at least face his attacker. The old man had seen what happened to his daughter and knew that biting wasn't an option, so he continued to clutch the squirming hero while searching for another point of attack.

After a brief hesitation—in his blind aggression—the zombie Dad began head-butting Claws violently in the face. Now Claws was a tough guy and had taken more than a few punches in his time so this attack, while painful, was doing far more damage to the man than he. Sure, the first few shots got Claws good and his confidence was shaken, but they also shattered his attacker's nose and eye socket. This was the flaw in the zombie self-defense system. It was rarely the measured or most elaborate approach, but employed for pure brutal 100% efficiency. Like curing a head cold with a blowtorch to the face, or stubbing your big toe and hacking it off with a machete. Right now the primal brain raging in this guy's head was screaming one message "hit, hit, hit, hit, GO!" So he was hitting with whatever he could.

As he smashed his face against Claws' granite-like cheekbones, splashes of blood continued to spray out as the old man further obliterated his own ugly mug. Eventually Claws began leaning to the back and sides to dodge the blows, more in disgust at the volume of bloodshed than through any pain. By this stage the zombie's bones were so crushed it just felt like being hit with a small sack of seeds.

This is when Claws saw—between the wildly thrashing head movements—the mother turn toward the knives and she readied to launch one in his direction. No sooner did it leave her hand, than Claws spun around to put the father in the firing line, and sure enough, the knife found a neat little spot to jam into his back. It must have done some damage because he relinquished his grip, which gave Claws some room to wriggle free. Another knife whizzed past their scuffle. Claws watched the father for a moment as he swung wildly with a definite loss of motor control, and waited for the wife to strike again. This time when she tossed her final blade across the room, Claws plucked the knife from the air, and ripped the other knife from the father's back, before using them to slice off his head in one clean hack.

As the air and bodily fluids mingled in the now un-capped esophagus of the zombie corpse, Claws returned his gaze to the wife who was holding his flail and experiencing quite a strong degree of bother as her husband slumped lifelessly to the floor. He paused for a moment, unsure how to react if she decided to lash out with his own weapon against him.

Meanwhile behind him, the brother silently rose to his feet with the table leg still sticking through his chest. As Claws took a step back away from the woman, he felt the table leg poke him in the lower back and closed his eyes painfully as the brother's heavy breathing crept closer to his ear.

"Oh, man, I hope that's just a knife in your pocket," he winced.

Claws looked over his shoulder at the impaled brother. It seemed he was indeed sporting some kind of wood, as Claws had feared, but thankfully just not the kind he need be overly concerned with at that point in time. He returned his gaze to the mother while talking back to the brother.

"Sorry buddy, as my wife would say—you've got two hands, take care of it yourself," Claws joked to hide the mounting fear and stress of this battle, which was going far worse than he had anticipated, and now he was surrounded! Claws couldn't take his eyes off the mother in case she charged with that flail, and the brother was proving a nuisance looming behind him despite a chunk of wood hanging out of his chest. Claws did his best to feebly swipe at the brother in his peripheral vision, but he just couldn't quite see him well enough to hit the target. It was like a twisted game of pin the tail on the donkey, only *he* was the one everyone was trying to stab. Inevitably, the brother managed to grab his arms and pulled Claws backwards to dig the wooden spike into his spine. Claws arched his back against the almost unbearable pain, but resistance made it worse, and left him merely a puppet for the brother to simply guide around the floor. The brother took a step forward toward his mother, which pressed the spike harder into Claws back and forced him to step forward as well, prodding him closer to the oscillating flail in the mother's grasp. Any confidence he had felt earlier was now all but gone.

Just inches from the mother, Claws mounted one final assault. With the wood digging into his back, he couldn't twist or fight against the brother's grip. His only option was to hop into the air, lifting his legs so his body lay horizontally in the air with his back now safely above the spike. He then kicked out with his legs, striking the woman in the chest and pushed off her to launch himself back in the direction of the brother. Their heads collided with a smack, and Claws rolled across the ground as the brother merely stumbled.

The brother regained his footing quickly and charged at Claws who was still kneeling on the floor trying to recover. Looking up just in time, Claws grabbed the stomach spike with one hand—just inches from his face—and with the other fist struck the young monster in the chest to halt his momentum. Claws then uppercut the spike to snap off the end before jamming it back into the brother's chest. With two wooden stakes now skewering the muscle-bound monster, Claws threw a punch to drop the young man to the ground. Well that was the plan anyway. Instead, the brother simply caught his fist and began crushing his knuckles in his palm. He spun Claws back into a headlock and turned him to face the mother again.

Claws was exhausted, trapped, and all out of ideas as he was frogmarched toward the matriarch of this little den. The mother gave a devilish smile as he drew nearer, raising the flail for one final swing until suddenly a dark ball of dirt hit her arm like a snowball and stuck to her bicep. She watched curiously as the dirt began to spread until her whole arm was as black as coal, then it dropped to the ground and shattered on the floor. Claws was stunned, as was the brother who released his grip and backed away.

Larry stood next to a bowl of fruit, he was bored now and ready to go home.

Suddenly several more dark bullets struck the woman, and more pieces of her disintegrating body turned to coal as they fell to the floor. As Claws watched the dissolving female, the impaled brother quietly pulled the wood from his stomach and readied to stab Claws. He raised the stake and thrust forward with such powerful fury that he would have drilled through a solid stone wall let alone Claws' relatively spongier physique. No sooner did the tiniest splinter find its way through his jacket and push a dent in the skin, did Ralph come crashing through the wall beside them and bite the brother around the waist. Claws spun just in time to see Ralph drag the young man into the yard where the other dragons set upon him, tearing him apart.

Claws looked around at the carnage of the house and breathed a sigh of relief. Suddenly he jumped as a volcano of blood erupted beside him. He'd forgotten all about the daughter whose head was now completely decayed from tasting his blood. Her heart—the same as the other monster before—exploded upon her demise.

With his clothes soaking red from the blood, Claws emptied a nearby sack of wheat and stuffed the decapitated husband inside to be dissected later. The dark elves wandered over to the body of the girl and applied their dark magic, turning her to the coal-like rock as well—though they saved a leg for the trip home, it was after all the tastiest part—before leaving so that none would know what evil had lurked in their town.

No sooner had Claws hoisted the sack over his shoulder, than he heard tiny footsteps coming down the staircase in the other room. He wandered over just in time to see an excessively cute five-year-old boy toddle down half asleep. The boy stopped at the bottom step and looked at Claws, rubbing his eyes.

"Who are you?" He quizzed innocently.

"Well, I'm... a friend," Claws smiled, but he felt far from convincing.

"What's in your bag?"

"It's..." Claws paused for a moment, trying to think of any other answer besides 'your dead father.' Eventually, he gave up. He put out his hand and readied to explain the gruesome truth to the child, when suddenly the father's heart exploded inside the bag and the toy snowman he'd been bludgeoning Claws with, fell out of the sack into his open hand. Claws looked at it for a moment before getting an idea.

"Why, it's a present for you. For... being such a good little boy all year," he lied.

The boy brightened. "Really?"

"Why, yes. I can tell... you know, when someone's been naughty or nice," explained Claws. He hadn't seen this much bullshit since his dad made him clean the barn about 20 years ago, but he just couldn't stop himself.

"Did my sister get a present? Coz she's always being mean to me," said the little boy.

"Oh, she got what was coming to her," quipped Claws, who had suddenly noticed Peter trying to wander into the hallway carrying the severed leg of the girl. "But don't you worry," he continued, subtly using his foot to push the young elf back into the kitchen. "You just head back up to bed and be really good and maybe I'll come back next year to check up on you."

"All right," said the boy cheerfully as he climbed back up the staircase.

"Oh, ho, hooooo," Claws coughed. "That's the way, to-morrow you'll wake up with lots of presents!" he beamed, before he turned toward the kitchen mumbling, "and a whole range of issues that'll probably scar you for life."

Claws returned to where Peter and Shirly were now at-tempting to reconstruct the sled with as much success as a four-year-old conducting brain surgery. "Larry, can you try and find some presents for that kid?" Claws asked. "Steal something if you have to coz his life just slipped straight down the shitter." He looked over to see Larry munching on the body of a stray animal.

"Oh Jeez, Larry!" he exclaimed. The elf looked up startled. "There's the icing on the cake right there. I get half eaten by a house full of monsters and that gives you the munchies." He was exhausted and slumped down against what remained of the sled. Shirly tapped him on the ankle and raised his flail for him to take. Claws smiled.

"But I do need to thank you guys, you really dragged my ass out of the fire there," Claws conceded, as Ralph also wandered over to receive his due recognition. "And, you too, you creepy monster," he smiled as he tousled his mane.

He looked at the scrapheap currently passing for a sled and shuddered at the thought of another trip like the one he'd endured on the way over. Suddenly, Claws had an idea. He ran back inside the house and headed upstairs with the dragons following behind him. He called to the kid who was curled up in bed with his bloody snowman and an excited grin on his face.

"Hey, kid, can I use your bathroom for a second?" Claws called.

After a few moments the roof of the house exploded as the dragons flew out with Claws seated inside a blackened bathtub and the legs of the zombie dangling from a sack in the back. His new vessel was far more aerodynamic and moved through the air with a greater zip and ease of control. He smiled as they soared up into the sky, while below the villagers had begun to gather in the streets—their natural curiosity drawing them toward the bloodied lair of the town's once most deadly secret. So much for his plan of subtle extraction.

"Now, let's see if I remember these names. On Dasher, on Dancer, on Prancer, and Vincent," he called as the team climbed higher. He leaned over to look at the names of the other dragons that he had not yet become acquainted with, but squinted to make out the bouncing nametags. "Um, Conner? And Quetip! And Boner, and Blitzen? What the hell did she call you guys?" he shouted. His outrage at the ridiculous roll call got him so worked up that he soon threw himself into another coughing fit. "Oh, ho, ho, ho, hooooo," he bellowed harder and harder until throwing up in the zombie bag and collapsing on the floor of the tub.

As he lay in the bathtub picking chunks of spaghetti from his beard, he thought about warning the other villagers about the hidden evil of their town. Then he plucked a particularly clean-looking piece of pasta from his chin and stared at it for a moment. He *was* hungry now. "Ah forget it," he rationalized. "They'll figure it out," before stuffing the regurgitated rigatoni back into his mouth.

With all the commotion, the young boy had sprung from his bed and ran to the window. Starry-eyed he stared up into the sky as his gift-giving friend sailed away through the skies in his sleigh pulled by the nine winged 'reindeer'. He wondered what other lucky kid might be visited next for a look in that sack, and he couldn't wait to tell his parents.

"Oh, ho, ho, ho, hooooo," the jolly man in red bellowed back, and the boy waved excitedly in hopes he'd be seen.

Meanwhile in the street below, a hooded figure limped through the crowd towards the semi-demolished homestead. He shouldered a young man aside who had begun furiously scribbling some world-changing sketches into a notebook as he watched Claws disappear. The bump jolted his book free, and it thudded to the ground. On the cover the man had etched his name, T. Nast, into the fabric—proving that even in a Christmas story you can still find the odd easter egg.

The limping figure made no apologies as he passed the vacationing artist. Eventually he removed his hood for a better look and rubbed his neck, which jingled as he disturbed a chain of claws that surrounded it. He sneered angrily at the sight of his ashen kinsmen within the house, and for a moment, his eyes began to fill with blood as his hand began to shake. He gripped his cane tightly to steady himself and calmly tucked his head back inside the hood. Then—once again consumed by his darker zombie alter-ego—gave one last hateful glance back up at the flying red menace before snarling and disappearing into the crowd.

Claws breathed a sigh of relief and tried to relax. It had been a hard night but at least this town was safe. He leaned forward and called out to his team, "OK, guys, let's go home." Soon the house disappeared from sight as they flew down the street. He settled back and shut his eyes, ready to indulge a restless nap filled with horrific memories of those nightmarish monsters. *Well, that's something to look forward to*, he sighed, then suddenly felt the tub dropping down again. They had only made it as far as the end of the street before the dragons crashed down on the roof of another house.

"What are we doing? Are you guys tired already?" he joked.

From inside the house, he heard a man's sleepy voice ask, "Hey, honey, did you hear something on the roof just then? Honey?"

There was a loud roar and the man screamed as Claws sighed with frustration, dragging himself to his feet. "Oh, I get it," he sighed as he stepped off the sled. "We're on again."

Suddenly one of the elves threw another clump of coal at Claws' feet and he watched as the patch of roof beneath him turned black. "So, what now? You want me to climb down their chimney?" he snapped sarcastically. He was tired and could feel he was getting grumpy.

Obediently, Larry hopped out and walked over to stand next to him. He paused for a moment and looked up at Claws in silence before stamping his foot down on the coal, which shattered, sending Claws crashing through into the house. The dark elves then set to work patching the hole while Claws began another scuffle below.

13

BAD SANTA

They say time heals all wounds, and sure, if you're the recently christened King of Christmas—with immortality gifted to you in the form of a lungful of dragon breath—the case could certainly be made at least for a superficially calculated clean bill of health. But the meaty mushy business floating around in your skull is a much more delicate instrument. Even taking into account the many horrors Claws had already endured in his lifetime, that first hunt was MESSED UP, and there were some deeply carved psychological wounds that a thousand years of rainbows and puppies wouldn't be able to bury down in denial.

There were still nights that Claws would wake in a sweat, seeing zombies hanging off his ankle and donkey kick Befana onto the floor. Now another popular saying is that hell hath no fury like a woman scorned. Well, as Claws found out, *no one* hath fury like a zombie-woman kicked out of bed in the middle of the night. Before Claws could even say "oops" he would feel the entire bed launch into the air and smash into the wall on the other side of the room with him somewhere inside the wreckage. Lucky, he wasn't a snorer.

Eventually, Claws found his way back to the old once-haunted house of the zombie toymaker, looking for some sense of closure. If anyone asked, he was there to see that the young boy had been safely rehomed, visiting of his own accord. But in truth Befana's insistence had finally worn him down, and he wouldn't be welcome back home until the boy was ok.

He stood in the yard, and stared at his nightmare. Its walls were still more hole than whole, and traces of their ashen corpses still wafted about the room despite weeks of time passing for this dust to settle. Claws had chosen a much less conspicuous outfit this time than the polar-bear fleece dripping with Homo sapien entrails he'd worn that fateful night. Just a casual checked shirt and cap, no flail. He looked like a lumberjack trying to make sense of the world outside his forest as he took in the scene and re-lived the painful memories.

"Can I help you?" smiled a man who looked way too pleased to see him as he wandered over and touched Claws' bulging bicep.

"Yeah," Claws fumbled for his question. "The kid who was here when the family…"

"Disappeared?" said the man, trying to finish his sentence for him.

"I was gonna say 'were ripped apart' but, yeah, that's a nicer way of putting it."

The man took a step back, somewhat shocked and disgusted by the crass yet handsome stranger. Then again, rugged untamed mountain men were kind of his type so what else did he expect? The man resumed his space-invading stance, practically latching on to Claws' hip like a conjoined twin, and met the hero's look of uneasy concern with a serial killer grin.

"Speaking of ripped," he cooed with a nervous energy. "How have I not noticed you around here before?"

Claws squirmed for a moment as he detached himself from his admirer. "I don't know," he groaned. "But if you give me a head start, I'll try make it harder next time."

"Promise?" said the man. Claws had to give the guy points for persistence. As much as the sex eyes he was getting made Claws' feel both dirty and disgusted, part of him felt strangely flattered by the attention. But he could never be interested. Could he? Suddenly Ralph wandered around the corner with Larry perched on his back as the man screamed mid-flirt. They were tired of waiting around for Claws to move things along. Plus it was seeming increasingly more likely that if Claws didn't pull his finger out soon, this guy was probably going to put one in.

Claws took his cue from the odd-looking intruders and steeled himself. "Right, the boy." Then to the man he snarled, "So where is he?"

The now-terrified man struggled to form his sentence, clearly distracted by Ralph as he snarled at him. "He's not here. Is your reindeer going to kill me?" he quivered.

Claws considered the idea for a moment before waving his hand for Ralph to relax. He sighed, this was supposed to just be a quick visit to check on a kid but between all the flirting with dudes and running around the countryside he wondered if he would ever get home.

Just then Ralph sneezed and the burst of flame proved the tipping point for the local who, understandably, fled the scene. "Great, now how are we going to find the kid," Claws shook his head with frustration.

"I don't recognize you stranger," an old man nearby wandered over to inspect the crew. He would have been somewhere in his 70s, big bushy white beard and straw sun hat. He looked like a farmer. Ralph growled at the intruder.

"Really?" Claws quizzed the old man sarcastically. "Was it the dragon or the demon elf that tipped you off?" His patience was done. He really didn't want to be there.

"It was the dragon," the old man shot back matter-of-factly. "Are you the one who took out those dead-beats?" he asked.

"The what?" Claws, thought he knew what the guy was talking about but didn't want to give anything away.

"You know, bloodshot eyes, frothing mouth, super strong. A ticking time-bomb of fury wrapped in a squishy skin suit of anger and stupidity," said the man. "Well most of 'em anyway."

"Yeah, you got it," Claws was sold. "We call them zombies. How long have you known about them?" He was intrigued to be able to finally discuss these things with someone else.

"Zombies eh? Oh years," the man replied, "They're so hard to spot though, it's no wonder people don't notice them."

"I know right? They seem to be everywhere, how does nobody see them?" Claws had been holding that question in for a while.

The old man wandered closer to the crew and began packing a pipe with dirt and sticks. "Because that's the truly beautiful part of the disease. They get up in the morning, kiss their kids goodbye, and push through the day-to-day doldrums of their meaningless lives with the same enthusiasm as any other idiot whose dreams of escaping the rat race have been crushed under the boot of reality. Singers cleaning toilets, writers selling houses, savants driving carts, and... zombies. That stinging slap in the face realization that you are destined to underachieve is as damaging to the mind as any death-bringing bacteria," he rambled.

Claws nodded along to the beat of his tale. This guy really got it. Everywhere Claws looked now he was paranoid that another zombie was lying somewhere just beneath the surface. He had so many questions. "So, what do you do out here?" Claws quizzed him curiously.

"I run zombie hunting expositions," he beamed.

"Don't you mean expeditions?" Claws corrected.

"Yeah, those too," the man grumbled, leaning on the fourth wall of the house. "So you're after the kid, huh? Here to finish him off?" This guy had zero emotional variance. All this time hunting zombies seemed to have sucked the life right out of him. *Is that how I'm going to end up?* wondered Claws.

"I just came to *find* the boy, actually, and make sure he's all right. I came over as soon as I heard," he lied. "I don't think he's a deadbeat, though, as you put it," said Claws, noticing that Ralph was getting more restless as the conversation wore on.

"You never can be too sure," the old man warned. "Kill 'em anyway is my motto. They can't kill you if they're already dead."

That was a much darker turn than Claws had expected, but the guy seemed to know his stuff. He extended his hand to the old man, saying, "I'm pretty new to this zombie hunting game. Any chance I could convince you to join me?" Claws had to hold Ralph still as something really stirred the young dragon.

"Got nothin' else to do, I guess," the old man shook his hand. Claws subtly pointed at Ralph and insisted he chill out. Ralph reluctantly settled and followed behind the two men as they began walking.

"So, any idea where the kid is?" Claws pushed again hopefully.

"On the edge of the forest. About one day north from here. It's a little shack over with his uncle. The guy is an absolute piece of dirt. Maybe you wanna kill him too?" Claws assumed the old man was joking, but his expression was sincere.

"I'm not killing anyone today if I can help it," Claws reiterated.

"Fine, so what else do you want to know?" the man conceded.

"Let's start simple. How do you spot these things?" asked Claws.

"Well, it's the stress that really makes them stand out," the man explained. "That's how you get 'em to turn. Really play on their emotions. Sometimes it's as simple as stealing their sandwich, other times you've just gotta keep chipping away at them until they change. That's how I found out my wife was a zombie," he seemed so casual as he slipped the comment into their conversation. "Turns out it's a very fine line between your heart jumping out of your chest, and wanting to rip out someone else's. But they're mostly careless by that point and it's easy enough to outsmart them."

"Wait, your wife was a zombie? Mine too!" Claws interrupted, surprised both at the fact *and* the casual nature by which it was introduced.

"Oh yeah, we both were. Just a couple of crazy kids killing whatever we liked. We really just let ourselves fall right into that lifestyle for a while. But, call it an occupational hazard if you will, but when you're digging that deep—like a fart gag gone wrong—things tend to get messy. And it did. I found her going after my dog one day. That crossed the line, so I killed her," he said.

Claws stopped dead in his tracks and replayed the last 20 seconds of the conversation in his head. Had he heard this guy correctly or was he losing his mind? One of them had to be crazy and Claws was pretty sure he was still barely holding his end together. He looked at the zombie slayer. Now what was he supposed to do? Or worse, what would he do if Befana just... gave in to the disease like this guy? Claws looked at Ralph, now realizing why the young dragon had been so distressed.

"So I'm just hunting alone now. If they look like a zombie, I don't ask questions, I just kill them," said the man.

"So, you're a zombie?" Claws confirmed. "And you kill zombies?"

The man nodded.

"But potentially normal people as well if they just look angry?" Claws pressed.

Claws was 90 percent sure this guy needed to die, but maybe he was just some misunderstood antihero. Maybe he had some redeeming quality. He WAS killing zombies after all...

"Or just grumpy, depressed, or I just get a feeling, you know?" the man chirped like a psychopath. "Never can be too careful."

His comments wiped any lingering sense of admiration Claws may have felt toward him as he was quite clearly insane. He signaled for Ralph to intervene, and the dragon snarled as he readied to attack. Within seconds the man transformed into his monstrous alter-ego and took a swing at Claws, but it did little to stop Ralph from enjoying an afternoon snack.

If nothing else, meeting this guy had given Claws a clearer understanding of what Befana was going through. The self-control she must have possessed to not just slit his throat every time he pissed her off—it must have been incredible. And that was before she even became a zombie. He chuckled to himself as an eyeball bounced off his leg.

As he looked down at the stray eye rolling in the dirt it reminded him of another comforting point surrounding her zombie-ism. If she did ever try to take out his pet, this one would probably win.

14

THE BIG BAD RALPH

C laws nodded to his team and jumped on Ralph's back as they set off. Ralph wasn't quite big enough to take his weight in the air for sustained flight, not yet, but a short gallop was certainly no issue and was far less conspicuous.

Ralph's blistering growth rate was still showing no signs of slowing down, by now he was already nearing the size of a regular horse. But Ralph was faster than a regular horse—his claws offered a little more grip to help push and turn—so it didn't take them too long to reach the shack that the old man had spoken of. There was a deep ravine that would have caused the biggest hold-up if they were to ride around it, but Ralph just spread his wings when no one was watching and glided over the gap.

They arrived to see the orphaned boy's uncle and his wife embroiled in some kind of domestic dispute out in the yard. The uncle had been chopping wood and now absent-mindedly swung the axe around as he waved his hands expressively during their argument. There were a few times he came within an inch of dicing the woman's voice box, but the old bird didn't flinch. In fact, she actually took a step closer as she punched the uncle in the arm.

From what Claws could decipher, they were arguing over money. Specifically, how much they could have earned for selling the young boy they'd just inherited instead of abandoning him in the forest. *Ah, shit*, thought Claws, *another detour*. He shook his head as his day spiraled into why-did-I-bother territory.

"Let me get this straight!" Claws shouted, blatantly interrupting the bickering pair as he wandered toward them. "I rescued a young boy from his undead, monstrous, flesh-eating family, in a town that, on a good day, looks like the ass-end of a wallowing hog. Then he gets shipped off to a 'regular' family to live out his days, and you would think for this kid, the only way from there is up. But I come all the way out here to check on him—feeling like a bit of a hero, I might add—only to find that option A, *staying* with the monsters, was actually the safer choice?"

The pair stared at him and shared a vacant expression before the uncle finally piped up. "What?"

Claws sighed again. He'd been doing a lot of that today. These people were idiots but he still needed information. "You're an asshole," he translated sharply. "Now where's the kid?"

"You mean Nick?" asked the man. "Who knows? They tried ta dump im on us an we can barely forda feed ourselves. We sent de kids ta go lose im in de forest over dere." He waved a hand towards the trees. "Wif any luck none of em'll come back."

"What the hell, Chucky?" his wife piped up. "If you wanted all of em gone we coulda made heapsa money an just sold em. Why don't you ever listena me?"

The thick twang of illiterate drivel took an extra few seconds to decipher but Claws soon got the message. Despite seemingly closing in on his target all morning, the carrot still dangled a few more inches from his nose, and now a trip into the woods was to be his next inevitable hurdle. As the pair resumed their nonsensical squabble he turned and rode toward the forest. One way or another this was going to be his last stop. If he couldn't find the boy soon enough, then Ralph was going to just burn down the forest and be done with it.

The woods were quite thick, and a slim winding trail was all that could wriggle its way through the trees. Claws had little trouble squeezing down the path, with Larry meandering behind, but Ralph took a different route wherever he could find space to push deeper into the darkness.

Claws jumped as a wolf howled somewhere in the distance, and turned to see if anyone had noticed, only to spot Larry standing there shaking his head. Well, he couldn't really tell if that's what he was doing, but he just got the impression that smug little prick was doing something sarcastic or disapproving. These kids must be either really brave or really dumb to be wandering this far into the darkness, he thought to himself. Though based on the two slack-jawed Neanderthals he'd left banging their singular IQ points together back at their hovel, he was pretty sure these apples didn't fall too far from that tree.

He was scared enough and he was almost indestructible.

Eventually Claws began to see the soft glow of a porch light up ahead. He didn't know who would possibly want to live out here, but he imagined they weren't getting an overly favorable return on their investment. Not much demand for gloomy shitholes in the middle of nowhere at the moment, so their property prices had probably flatlined.

In any case he thought he might as well ask if they had seen the kid, so he stepped out into the clearing and marched toward the door. Not two steps into the clearing he suddenly heard a young child scream from inside the house before a huge wolf smashed its way out through a nearby wall. This thing was massive—easily bigger than a grizzly bear. Claws would have compared it more to the size of a minibus if they had been invented yet, but for now the word 'massive' would have to suffice.

The beast stood stock still for a moment, looking very bloated and pleased with itself. A tiny red hood dangled from its jaw, flapping in the breeze. Suddenly, it spotted Claws and snarled. While it already looked quite engorged, he was sure the great mutt would find room for a burly adventurer in its flea-ridden gut.

Strangely enough, for the wolf anyway, this tiny idiot wasn't backing down. Everything it had ever encountered all its life had run from it—its parents had even run away when a genetic or hormonal malfunction must have sent its growth rate into overdrive. So what was this two-legged tidbit hiding?

The wolf hesitated, trying to figure out the odd behavior of its dessert. Eventually its instinct re-engaged and the massive animal took a menacing step toward Claws.

Claws wasn't overly worried. He'd fought bigger creatures than this with flame-throwing optional extras included, so a big dog was certainly not as much of a threat. He reached for his flail but felt only the tattered holes in his baggy old pants leading him to two startling revelations.

> 1. He'd left his favorite weapon with the sled and dragons way out on the other side of town to avoid suspicion.

> 2. He needed some new pants.

A tiny bead of sweat rolled down his forehead as he considered hand-to-razor-sharp-jaw combat with a 10000-pound wolf. That same bead of sweat then trickled into his eye and the salt really stung for a moment. *Not a great start*, he thought.

He watched the wolf edge closer through some rapid eye-clearing blinks, with enough bricks quickly filling his pants to construct a small two-bedroom unit. *Maybe that's where all the holes were coming from.* Just then Ralph took a few casual steps out from the bushes to stand between his master and the beast. It would have been such a badass moment if Claws hadn't spotted him chasing butterflies just moments ago but, still, he was glad to have him.

This time it was Ralph's turn to stare menacingly at the wolf, with flames rising in his throat. Ralph was giving up a considerable weight advantage in the fight, but his power and speed went a long way to at least levelling the playing field.

The wolf had apparently never seen a dragon before, but it also didn't seem to care. By Claws' reckoning, the murderous canine was big enough to swallow the kid almost whole, and if it had, he had about five minutes left to get it out before the gastric juices and noxious gases caused irreparable burns and brain damage.

"Get him, boy," was all the encouragement the young dragon needed to spring into action. He leapt forward as the great wolf snapped shut its jaw, but Ralph spread

his wings and flew just inches past its head. Ralph landed behind the wolf and slashed its hind leg before it had
a chance to turn, yet the dragon's impressive wingspan
trailed behind him and still waved within range of his foe.
As Ralph readied a fireball in his throat, the wolf latched
onto the tip of a wing and reefed the little dragon across
the ground, sending it tumbling and smashing into some
bushes.

The dragon jumped to its feet and shook itself, but was
quickly set upon again by the wolf who bit hard into his
shoulder and pinned him up against the tree. Claws was
not about to let Ralph do all the heavy lifting as he ran
in to help. He sent a heavy right hook into the wolf's jaw,
causing it to let go and turn its head toward Claws.

The wolf nipped at him a few times as Claws ducked
and rolled back and forth, buying time for the dragon to
regain its footing. Ralph tried to blast some fire but could
only manage a spark. So instead, he made a wing-assisted
lunge onto the back of the wolf and found some sweet
revenge as, this time, he was the one to sink his teeth into
his opponent's shoulder. Though the giant beast growled
in pain, it still managed to latch onto its secondary target
of Claws.

The wolf bit down on Claws' abdomen—one of its teeth
nearly puncturing his lung. The sudden pressure winded
him, and Ralph's swiping and nipping was doing little

to slow down the beast. The dragon continued to throw sparks like a faulty wire, but still couldn't manage a flame.

Claws was struggling for air as the wolf smashed him into the ground time after time. During one hit, a large stick went straight through Claws' leg, and he roared with agony, however, it did give him an idea. Then the wolf whacked him again and his head struck a rock.

He forgot his idea.

As he flailed about in its jaws, dazed and trying to work out what was going on, he wondered what the pain was in his leg. Meanwhile, Ralph had now jumped off the wolf's back and grabbed its hind leg in his jaws. Ralph bit with enormous pressure and felt the bone snap, similar to the sounds coming from Claws' chest as his ribcage gave way.

Claws ran a shaky hand down to where the pain was coming from in his leg to find a stick poking through it. *Oh, yeah.* He finally remembered his idea as the wolf threw him in the air and roared from the pain of its own freshly broken leg. In the brief moment of weightlessness—as Claws' momentum shifted from upward to downward motion, several feet in the air—he ripped the stick from his leg and then jammed it straight into the wolf's eye as he fell back down to Earth.

His feet barely had time to touch the ground when the wolf kicked him heavily in the face with its good leg, and he sailed across the clearing into a tree. The beast then turned and grabbed Ralph by the base of his throat and ripped him off its leg before slamming him into the ground. The wolf shook him like a squeaky chew toy as Ralph struggled to fight back. Claws tried to get up but there were a lot of owies his body was trying to heal, and it was going to be a few minutes before he was even a chance of moving his arm.

As Ralph's growl turned to a whimper, it wasn't looking good. Claws could only watch as the young dragon sprayed blood like a broken sprinkler until at last, with one final shot of energy Ralph turned his head toward the wolf's and blasted a long, strong burst of flame, scorching the hair and skin from the great animal's head.

The wolf stumbled backwards. It was a mess. Ralph now climbed to his feet, still a little wobbly but sensing his moment to finish the job. He charged at the wolf, putting a heavy shoulder into its ribcage as the beast stumbled once more. Then he carved a deep gash in each of its front legs, which buckled under the weight as the damaged tendons no longer offered any support.

Ralph spread his wings and leaped into the air. He landed on the wolf's head, his front claws gripping it behind the jaw and his rear legs pushing down on its shoulders. With a great strain punctuated by another huge fireball, Ralph ripped the wolf's head from its shoulders—the spine spewed endlessly from the bloody head hole like a clown offering someone a trick handkerchief.

Eventually Ralph placed a foot on the spine to snap it from the skull then tossed the now-homeless cranium in the direction of Claws. Ralph snarled for a moment at the corpse in case there was some chance of reanimation—after all, he'd seen this often enough in the humans—but after a few moments of stillness, he relaxed.

Claws sat for a moment taking in the event before he suddenly remembered his mission. "Oh crap, the kid!" He hauled his battered body off the ground and stumbled over to the wolf's head. With a quick twist of his semi-functioning arm, he ripped the largest tooth from the mouth of the beast and ran back to the torso to begin hacking into its bulging stomach. The hide was thick, but the tooth was razor-sharp, and ripped through the internal layers in no time just as it had done to Claws' tattered flesh moments earlier.

As the stomach contents spilled onto the grass, he searched through the remains of a torn-up old woman before finding a small girl buried under some limbs. She had largely been swallowed whole, but her arms and legs were a little chewed—must have been a little too big even for a wolf of that size to fit in its mouth. Her skin, particularly around her face, was burnt red from the harsh acids of the digestive system. More importantly, she wasn't breathing—no doubt she suffocated on the way down.

For a moment Claws sighed in defeat. It wasn't the boy he had hoped to rescue but he still felt sorry for the young life lost. Or was it? He had heard about a technique called mouth-to-mouth resuscitation, something they were trying in France a while back and thought he'd give it a go. If she needed air, why not just give her some? The idea made sense and was simple enough. He leaned down and began blowing air into her lungs, watching her little chest rise and fall. He had no idea what he was doing, but something was surely better than nothing.

Just then her eyes shot open and she began screaming and coughing violently. His inept mouth-to-mouth may have been uncoordinated, but he had forgotten the kicker that swung the odds considerably in favor of success. The gas. Her arm must have been broken as he heard the tightening muscles and tendons snap it back into place while her skin sizzled and healed a little. The chewed limbs also sewed themselves up to a crisscrossing of scars. When she finally stopped screaming and her breathing had calmed, Claws put a caring hand on her shoulder, "Are you OK?"

No sooner had his hand touched her shoulder than the young girl lashed out with a tiny fist that deflected his arm and whacked him in the nose. It wasn't hard but was just enough to get the eyes watering. She jumped back to retrieve the tattered red hooded cape from the ground and swung it over her shoulders. As it billowed around and settled onto her frame she stared him down. It would have made for an intimidating stance were she at least 15 years older, but all he saw was a cute little seven-year-old girl playing dress-ups.

"I know what you did, and thanks," she growled seriously. "But don't ever touch me again."

Claws just smiled. *So cute*, he thought. He took a second to assess her injuries. From a distance, of course. The burns on her skin had largely healed except a large patch across her face. Her limbs seemed to move freely but still bore the scars where the wolf had chewed her up. A portion of her brown hair had a few bleached streaks through it where the acid burn must have been too bad to fully heal with the limited power of his breath. Still, she seemed fine. "And what's your name, little girl?" he asked, inadvertently mocking the super-cool vibe she was trying to lay down.

"Call me Hood," she growled again.

Just then Ralph nudged him feebly for some love, and Claws turned to give him a pat and check over his battered body. By the time he looked back, the girl had disappeared. For a second he was startled and impressed, until he heard her scrambling up a nearby tree. He watched her for a moment trying to throw her leg over a low-hanging branch, and almost offered to help but he thought he'd let her have her moment after everything she'd just been through. Eventually she got over the branch before slowly crawling the rest of the way up the tree. Once there, she found a high enough perch and sat hidden, watching them from above until they left.

15

NICK OF TIME

C laws groaned with every hobbling step he trudged through the forest. His healing factor was working overdrive to get his body back in order, and he could see Ralph suffering a similarly painful skeletal realignment with his mangled wings cracking and twisting.

Just then Larry wandered over, his arms full of breadcrumbs that he was casually stuffing into what could only be assumed was a mouth. "Thanks for all your help back there," Claws bellowed sarcastically.

Larry clicked back at Claws to shut up, warning that if he didn't, then when he finished his snack, he was going to start on a main course of big stupid human.

Claws smiled ignorantly, "No I'm not mad at you, you just need to be a little more mindful of what's going on around you. I accept your apology." Claws was quite pleased at how quickly he had picked up their language and made friends with this strange little race. *I'm nailing this*, he mused.

With each passing minute his body started to feel marginally better, and his stride improved. He was certainly getting hungry now too, as the running repairs had heightened his metabolism, which now required larger snack sizes to fuel the fire. He considered trying to steal some of Larry's crumbs, but he had already seen the elven nightmare eat some pretty horrible things already, so who knows where he had found them.

"Where did da crumbs go?" Came the irritated voice of an arrogant young boy from outside the clearing.

"How shud I know?" A girl shot back defensively. "Weren't you supposta be droppin em?"

"I did, I've been doin it all da way to her house," said the boy, who looked like he was about 12 years old.

"Didn't I tell ya it waza stupid idea? There are so many animals in ere that would eat em. Use rocks. O'course, they were neva gonna stay there." Her I-told-you-so moment was being buried under the mounting stress.

Claws looked at Larry who paused for a moment before continuing to eat his stolen treats.

"OK, so we got no trail an no idea which way ta get out. Whatta we do?" asked the boy who was beginning to adopt his sister's stress.

"I bet Nick hid em," she growled. "That little brat!"

"No wonder Dad wanted im gone," said the boy.

This was enough to pique Claws' interest. "Excuse me," he interrupted with significantly more subtlety than his earlier run-in with their parents. Though subtlety is a difficult art when you suddenly emerge next to them through some bushes. "I'm just passing and heard you say you were dumping a young boy somewhere. Any clue as to where that might be?"

The children were silent for a moment. Not through fear, but more like a couple of criminals caught standing in an empty vault trying to think of another reason why they're holding bags of cash. But like the mermaid in a shoe store, Claws just wasn't buying.

"Perhaps I wasn't clear enough," said Claws, lowering his tone. "I just pulled a little girl from the stomach of a big bad wolf, which I killed with the help of my pet dragon. Now am I going to have to add two brat kids to my list or are you going to answer the question? Where's the kid?"

It was the boy who cracked first, invoking a disapproving sneer from his sister. "Our dad made us do it," he whined. "I didn't mind im but Dad said we couldn't afforda keep im so we took im to the wi..."

"The woman in the forest," the young girl suddenly piped up, cutting her brother off. He looked surprised by the interruption, but she frowned at him again and he shut up. "Isn't that right, Hansel?"

The boy nodded suspiciously. Clearly they were keeping something from Claws but he was an immortal monster-killer with a dragon and some kind of demon as a sidekick. He could handle the antics of a few jerk kids and a forest-dwelling hippie.

"Fine, show me," he sighed, signaling to the path ahead. "And I'll try not to act too surprised when you drop a bucket of water on my head or whatever prank you two are planning to hit me with when we get there."

As it turned out, gloomy middle-of-nowhere shitholes must have been becoming something of a trend because it wasn't long before they saw another porch light up ahead. This time Claws was a little more cautious as he stepped into the clearing, but his mind was instantly put at ease when he caught a glimpse of the house. Candy canes, shortbread, marshmallow, toffee—this place was a sweet tooth's dream and a diabetic's worst nightmare.

The roof was shingled with shortbread, glazed with a hard sticky toffee that glistened in the sun. Biscotti boards panelled the house, held by choc chips shaved into pointy nails, beaten into the sides. The window frames had a swirl to their shape, like dollops of white chocolate ganache spread around the sugar glass panes. From pillar to post, everything was edible, and he could just feel the calories piling onto his ass as he breathed in a gust of orange sherbet that sprinkled down from the roof. *What kid would want to be saved from this magical place?* He thought. *Hell, if she made up an extra bed I'd move in as well.*

Claws nibbled a small chunk of the shortbread fence as he wandered up to the house in a drunk-like stupor. He turned to look for the kids but saw them bolting in terror back down the path out of sight. *Strange*, he thought. He wandered casually over to the window to get a look inside and could smell the white-chocolate glaze on the walls as he leaned against them so as not to be seen. He noticed a small drizzle of the gooey white goodness dribbling down the wall and he couldn't resist scooping a little bit off with his finger. Whether the house was melting or just freshly coated, he didn't care as he peered inside.

He could see an old lady sleeping by a fire, her knitting had fallen from her lap to the floor, and a birdcage hung nearby. Claws casually dipped his white chocolate-coated finger into his mouth as he scanned the room and no sooner did the sweet liquid hit his tongue—*NOPE that was bird shit*. He gagged loudly outside the house, followed closely by uncontrollable hurling straight into her freshly trimmed garden bed. All the colors of the regurgitated rainbow spewed from his lips. This unfortunately, was not the first time he had eaten another creature's refuse, but it was certainly the worst. But that was a story for another time.

Eventually he was able to return to his feet, now violently scrubbing his tongue with a piece of candied drainpipe. He looked back up to see if, by chance, his outburst had not woken the woman, but her chair was empty, and the birdcage swung wildly. She must have bumped one of the legs as she passed it. *Wait*, he thought as his concern intensified. *Why are there human legs hanging from the birdcage? Oh, that's why the kids ran away.*

"Who are you?" came the sudden interrogation, which wrenched Claws from his thoughts.

"Oh, hi," Claws said, trying to smile innocently as he faced the ragged old bird who was standing in the doorway. "I was just admiring your lovely…" he froze like those stupid kids earlier, trying to think of an innocent reason as to why he would be standing so close to her window sucking on a piece of her house. "… garden?" he squeaked, with the confidence of any one of that numbskull family trying to spell the word 'illiterate.'

Of course, his mention of the garden also served to draw her attention to the fresh pile of vomit he'd recently deposited there, and she turned up her nose as the smell began to spread. "And is that my drainpipe?" she continued—man, he just could not catch a break.

Luckily a timid "Hello" from inside the house soon broke the tension and Claws remembered why he was there. He ran inside to find young Nick sitting sleepily in a cage.

"Don't worry buddy, I'll have you out of there in a second," he said trying to comfort the boy as he searched for something to bend the bars. They were sticky, like most things in this place, and sweet too. *Licorice, score!*

As promised, the boy was out in seconds and Claws carried him to the door with a handful of licorice for the trip home. However, as they approached the doorway, the old woman blocked their path. She looked pissed, and fair enough, he hadn't been the best house guest. *But, then again, she did kidnap a child, so we'll call it even,* he thought.

"You're not going anywhere," she snarled menacingly.

Claws smiled as he admired her confidence. "Sure thing, lady," he grinned, as he moved to ease her out of the way. But when he placed a hand on her shoulder she didn't budge. He pushed harder than he cared to admit, but it was like she was carved from marble and glued to the floor. Then, without warning, she reached her other hand up and grabbed his shirt. In the split second before he was hurled across the room, Claws called to Ralph and tossed the young boy through the doorway. Ralph dived forward and snatched him from the air, curling a wing around him to shield him in case of further attack but the door was slammed shut behind him.

Claws shook his head for a moment as he peeled himself from a freshly dented cupboard. That old woman had quite an arm on her. Slowly the world began to realign in his brain and the spinning stopped as he watched the woman cup her hands to her mouth. "Hugo!" she called out, then cackled maniacally before turning toward Claws. "Hugo should be along shortly to say hello. I was hoping for a more tender cut of meat for dinner, but I guess you'll do."

Claws waited for the other dinner guest to arrive and could see the woman growing more concerned with each minute that passed. Eventually she noticed the smears of blood on his clothes and stared more intently. "Hugo is never this late. Where did that blood come from?"

Claws climbed to his feet, raising his arms defensively. "Whoa, I didn't kill your husband if that's where you're going with this. There are plenty of other things out here that could do that. Case in point, this massive wolf I ran into trying to eat your neighbors."

"A wolf?" she spat. "Where is it?'

"I'm fine, thanks for asking," Claws mocked. "He nearly killed me until Ralph ripped his head off."

"Arrrgh!" she screeched, enraged by the revelation as green bolts of electricity pulsed across her body.

"Oh, that was Hugo, wasn't it?" groaned Claws, dreading what was probably to follow.

The woman blasted a bolt of the green energy at Claws. He tensed his body, bracing for impact, but it narrowly sailed past his head. He could still smell it burning through the air as he finally managed to squeeze a gap between his eyelids, and then his panicked expression turned to confusion. The woman was now smiling. "Don't worry," she chuckled. "I wasn't aiming for you."

Claws turned to see a mouse sitting on the cupboard glowing green. A snake had been approaching it for a feast until suddenly the rodent began growing to the size of a small bear, and the snake retreated in terror. The woman—actually, I think it's a pretty safe bet that we can now just call her a witch—pointed at Claws, and the mouse sprang into action. The green glow dissipated from its fur, and the creature looked kind of cute as it crawled towards our hero, well, except for the fact that its teeth were as big as his hand.

The mouse hopped and nipped at Claws as he stumbled away. It swiped its furry hands or feet, or whatever you're supposed to call them. It doesn't matter, he wasn't a scientist. Let's just say those things it walks on—they were trying to scratch him. But it was surprisingly slow, probably because its neural pathways and nervous systems were now stretched further apart than in its smaller form, so the signals were taking a little longer to travel around its body. So, Claws easily dodged it a few times, but his countering kicks and strikes seemed to annoy it more than injure. In reply, the mouse began baring those fangs and even managed to slice a hole right through his shoe and expose his toes to the cold. Good grief, his nails were dirty. When was the last time he'd bathed? It was concerning, both the giant mouse and his bathing situation, but for now he felt he could handle them.

Outside, the young boy had recovered from whatever spell the witch had cast upon him and wandered around the house inspecting his former prison, snacking on the various exterior furnishings and fittings. He could hear the odd bang and some swearing coming from inside, but he didn't really care, he was having a great time. Suddenly, a girl with a dark-red hooded cloak jumped from the roof and stood inches from his face. She looked coldly into his eyes, like a big cat defending her territory.

The boy smiled innocently. "Wanna play?"

He reached out to the girl—fingertips grazing her hood—but she immediately stepped back defensively and growled through gritted teeth, "Don't touch the hood."

The boy was unshaken and continued to stare. She was the most beautiful girl he'd ever seen. Once again, he pushed out a hand, and this time tapped her on the shoulder. "Tag," he squealed and squirmed on the spot. Hood's face reddened with rage.

The squealing and squeaking of the giant mouse concealed from Claws the commotion that ensued outside. Not that he could have got out there to help anyway.

The witch wasn't taking any chances with just one monster. Since her first baby had already bitten the dust, she raised her green glowing fist once more and hurled another blast toward the corner of the room. Suddenly a wolf spider emerged from the shadows, similar in size to the mouse, but so much more terrifying. Claws' heart skipped several beats as the new threat leapt in his direction. As Claws frantically retreated to dodge the arachnid, he tripped backwards over a chair and caught a pouncing mouse as he fell backwards onto the ground. His momentum launched the rodent over his head and into a wall before catching the spider on his feet as he lay on his back. For good measure the witch hit it with another bolt of green and it doubled in size again. Three rows of eight horrifying eyes stared into his soul as he held back the beast, but its body weight slowly pushed its fangs closer to its prey.

Claws' legs quivered under the sustained pressure, and he searched for a weapon to fend off the threat, but each time he reached for a suitable stick, one of the arachnid's limbs would stamp down on his own until he was left helplessly pinned and waiting below the beast. He could see drips of venom glistening on its fangs as they opened to clamp down on his throat. Claws squirmed but to no avail. He was done for.

Suddenly, a knitting needle zipped past his face and struck the creature in its own. It hesitated for a moment before the needle came back knocking several of its legs out from under it and it tumbled off to one side. Claws rose to his feet to see Larry now standing protectively between himself and the spider. Perhaps he had snuck in before the gingerbread door was slammed shut or simply ate his way through it during the commotion. Who knows? This place wasn't exactly Fort Knox given the deliciousness of its design, so that probably wasn't overly difficult. Right now, Claws was just glad to see the pint-sized protector standing guard for a friend, and he kind of felt bad about calling him a prick earlier.

Meanwhile, Larry was steeling himself for the creature's second assault as it groggily regained its footing. Battle was often not something he could really be bothered with, but Befana would not be happy if he let her companion be destroyed. Like a cockroach, the human fool was demonstrating an entertaining knack for defying death, but he was in way over his head this time. Magic was elf business, and while the witch showed considerable talent for a human, it was time she learned what true power lay within a master's grasp. Also, he was getting hangry, and Claws was taking too long.

Claws watched for a moment as Larry skillfully danced around the spider, commanding the needle like King Arthur's sword, parrying its strikes and striking its legs as it scurried about the floor. The needle may not have been sharp, but Larry struck with enough force to jam it through its exoskeleton, slowly dismantling the beast like a death by a thousand cuts.

Eventually the mouse began to recover, having been knocked senseless when it slammed its head into a heating grille. It now looked to rejoin the battle just as the spider was nearing its end. The witch was growing tired of Larry's meddling and her rage, once again, began to grow. This time a purple hue engulfed her body as the green had done before. She locked on to Larry and readied to send a thunderbolt in his direction.

"Larry, jump!" Claws screamed, shriller than he had hoped, as a purple bolt nearly clipped his friend. But the dark warrior obediently leapt into the air, and so instead, the purple blaze continued past, striking the mouse as it charged back into the fray. The mouse was instantly halted. It twisted, as if in pain, and then its body slowly hissed and melted away like the zombie girl had done when tasting Claws' blood. Within seconds it was a pile of ooze on the ground, and not long after, Larry plunged the knitting needle into the brain of the spider to grant them all a brief moment of peace. Larry tossed the needle aside and now turned his attention to the witch.

She was still sporting her purple death haze, but Larry seemed unfazed. They stared at one another like Old Western gunmen readying for a duel. Claws didn't know whether he could, or even should, help out but he didn't get long to decide. As if a switch was suddenly flicked, the witch launched several purple bolts at the little shadow who reacted by firing dark pellets of his own to blunt her attack. As the two colors collided, explosions sprayed glowing purple coal across the room, which burned through whatever surface it landed on. Claws dived under a table to avoid the debris and continued to jump from hiding place to hiding place as each one decayed.

Meanwhile, Larry and the witch were in full battle swing. Purple bolts fired at the elf who would dodge, block, and fire—unleashing his own arsenal right back at the ghastly old hag. Their back and forth continued with neither really gaining ground. This only heightened the witch's anger, and her attacks grew more intense with every deflection by the tiny elf until at last, consumed by rage, the woman ripped Claws' dented cupboard from the wall and threw it at Larry.

With ridiculous reflexes, Larry coolly tossed another coal pellet at the back of the cupboard, which was fast approaching. The coal spread across the surface, just as he had done to many zombie rooftops to allow Claws

access. As he burst through the back and unexpectedly, out the front doors of the cupboard unscathed, the
witch was taken by surprise, affording him one clear shot
with a swift black ball of coal. It sailed across the room
through the shower of glowing purple pellets and smacked
into her forearm as it pulsed with energy. The witch
shrieked—more at her frustration at being caught out,
than from the burning pain now tearing through her left
arm—but before the black death could spread and con-
sume her, she punched her fist through a nearby sugar glass
window and dropped her arm on a jagged shard to tear the
poisoned limb from her body. The arm fell to the ground
as the coal continued to entomb the pound or so of flesh.
But she paid it no attention. She wanted the elf.

The witch stared at Larry, panting as her toxic blood
pooled beneath her mangled bicep on the floor. Larry was
relatively pleased with how the battle was going. He was a
little rusty, if he was being honest, but he was impressed
by the magic human's extreme countermeasures. *Maybe
we could keep her too*, he considered. Suddenly she sent
another purple fireball in his direction as she resumed her
attack. *Nah, too angry*, he thought as he bounced away to
safety.

The room was crumbling around them amid burning
acid drops and disintegrating charcoal missiles, but every
now and then the witch upped the ante on her relentless
assault, firing the odd green bullet at the chandelier or

ceiling tiles that would rain down two, or even three times their size. Her missing hand didn't seem to diminish her magic in that arm, and if anything, it probably opened it up a little more with some fast balls really flying from the wound.

The dark elf, not to be outdone, spread a big chunk of coal above his head like a pizza-maker spinning his dough to catch the falling debris. He expertly fended off a few tiles as he rolled away from another bolt before launching his spinning shield across the room like the First Avenger. It smashed the witch right in the guts and she buckled over in pain. She wheezed for a moment as she removed it from her chest then stood up and snapped the shield over her knee. She frisbeed the first half up over Larry's head and just as it passed directly above him, she hit it with a few bolts of green causing it to grow big and plummet down upon him.

Larry caught the shield fragment but was struggling just to hold the immense weight of it above his head. Before Claws could help, the witch then spun the second piece of the shield low and straight at the little elf. Again, a few bolts of green added considerable size and Larry could do nothing but wait for this freight train to smash into him as he smiled beneath the first piece she had thrown. It had been a long time since another creature had bested him in combat. *What a lovely surprise,* he thought, before the second piece smashed into his stomach.

The little elf was knocked soundly unconscious as he hurtled across the room, oddly pleased by his unlikely defeat. This time Claws was quicker to react and dived toward the tumbling elf, grabbing him seconds before he was to be crushed between the spinning piece of coal and some large shortbread biscuit paneling. Claws laid him in the corner and inspected the diminutive hero. Somehow, he was still breathing.

Claws looked up at the witch, who smiled again knowing her victory was imminent. She spied the snake warily returning to search for more food. Claws spied the knitting needle Larry had dropped not far from his feet.

The witch fired up a massive green ball of flame and sent it on its way intending to deliver one enormous reptile ready to devour the boys. But with reflexes that surprised even himself, Claws dived toward its flight path, collecting the needle on his way and at full stretch javelined it back through the approaching bolt in the direction of the witch. As the needle passed through the green ball of energy, it collected a distinct glow, making it grow larger and larger until an Olympic-sized pole punched a satisfying void straight through her chest and pinned her to the wall. If she had ever possessed any scrap of a heart in that cantankerous corpse, it was now likely scattered somewhere out on her lawn.

Claws watched as the little snake timidly made its way toward the chunks of meat. *Hey, look on the bright side lady,* he thought, *at least now your snake finally has something to eat.*

Exhausted and in pain, Claws gently tucked Larry into his arms and headed for the door. He still had no idea of Hood's run-in with the boy, but as he neared the door, he could definitely now hear the screams. Claws practically kicked the door off its hinges as he jumped outside and scanned for the boy. He did not just come all this way out here to lose this game on the buzzer. To his surprise, young Nick *was* running, but the screams were coming from a smiling, joyful Hood as the pair happily chased one another across the yard.

Claws breathed a deep sigh of relief as he wandered over to them. He tousled Nick's hair lovingly as he passed him. "Glad to see you're feeling better," he chirped. Claws smiled down at the young girl whose hood was pushed back to reveal a scarred yet happy face. "And you too Little Red Hood. You wanna come back with us? I can try and find a better home for both of you."

As soon as Hood saw him, she stopped, pulled the hood back up to cover her head, and resumed her former icy stance. "The name's Hood," she shot back flatly. "And I work alone." She looked back at Nick who was still smiling at her, and as she watched him, a smile began to creep onto her face once again. As soon as she realized, she glanced at Claws, almost embarrassed by her temporary acquiescence to her humanity, before sprinting back into the forest.

Claws shrugged and sat down on the grass watching Nick playing innocently with Ralph, bounding along merrily together. He wondered how long it had been since he was that blissfully happy. When did he get so old? As he leaned against the house, he felt the earth warm beneath him. He plucked a chocolate cookie from the side of the garden bed and smiled. Still, life was pretty good.

Of course, he was actually sitting in his earlier vomit, which was slowly seeping through into his pants—hence the warmth—and the 'chocolate cookie' now nearing his mouth was really just a dead stink bug. But he didn't know that. So, at least for the next few seconds, Claws was happy.

16

ALL I WANT FOR CHRISTMAS...

News of Claws' first big zombie slaying night on the town had travelled far and wide, and a drawing by the young man from the crowd painted a very familiar picture. So, the story of the jolly red giant began to take shape and forever add a holiday asterisk to the concept of stranger-danger that plus-sized shopping center wannabes would dine out on for years.

Claws didn't know exactly what he was killing back then. Between Befana and the crazy zombie guide, he had a basic rundown of the science in general, but the mythology of zombies was still in its infancy. All he knew for sure was that they were evil and needed to be dealt with, and with the help of those elves and his 'flying reindeer' he got pretty good at it. Of course, the dragons had a far more acute sense for sniffing out the dead than he ever could, but in time Claws learned to hone his own senses as well. Once he got close to a town, he knew who'd been naughty or nice that year.

Those who saw the man at work needed some kind of explanation for what they were seeing, and daemons seemed to rightly fit the bill. His 'exorcisms' became so popular that people started calling him Santa, which roughly translated to 'holy' or 'saint' in a couple of languages. There is some debate as to whether Santa was actually the feminine form of the word and so he should have technically been called *San* Claws, but he was still just chuffed at the recognition.

The Dutch managed to piss off Larry as they too fleshed out their Christmas folklore. They called the mysterious elven creatures *Zwarte Piet* or 'Dark Pete', which Larry considered a sign of ignorance on their part, since he was clearly the one doing all the work. He assumed Peter had spread this propaganda just to annoy him, and so their relationship became somewhat strained.

As terrifying a concept as the zombie was, it didn't take long for it to find its way into mainstream culture either. The zombie lore certainly improved over time as more sightings helped to strengthen the story, and soon books and films would start parading them around as 'fictional' monsters. Idiots.

Santa set up shop in the North Pole among the spirit tribe of elves. Well, the actual North Pole sits somewhere in the middle of the Arctic Ocean where floating ice shelves will infrequently pass over the fabled spot. So, their floating village is as close as anyone could get to actually living there. Parents selfishly fueled the 'coal for the naughty, presents for the nice' myth that had begun that fateful night when Claws killed a family. But this tradition was as much a cop-out to keep their kids in line as it was a sign to the bearded reaper that they were still human and caring for their young.

Either way, Santa let them have their lie. Whatever the intentions behind their gift-giving, at least it was protecting the children from the harsher truth that the carbonized chunks of rock left behind for the naughty, were actually the remains of the naughty themselves—which, of course, were near-undetectable monsters who looked just like their mom and dad. Now what parent wants to read that bedtime story to their kid?

Eventually, Befana learned to control her own urges enough to get out of the house. She still didn't want to risk going out on the hunts in case she let loose. So, instead, she earned a reputation of her own by quietly taking presents to the odd kids that missed out during Christmas because their parents were either zombies or just didn't really care about maintaining the myth. You have to remember that there are many terrifying creatures out there—Frosty, the Easter Bunny, leprechauns and Mother Nature to name a few. And the little white lie is a powerful weapon against widespread fear and panic.

As the dragons got bigger, the sleigh grew too, and the hunts went longer. Claws would ride into town, as he stood astride the seat of the sleigh with flail in full swing and the dragon claws jingling around his neck.

Santa also had a son, or adopted one anyway, who was following in the old man's footsteps with unsurprising success. And a damn fine young man, if I do say so myself. As dangerous as he was handsome, which meant for women and zombies alike, when he set his sights on you, there was no escape. Although young is a bit of a stretch—he's about 130 now by my count—but looks good for his age thanks to a little dragon magic.

Yet even with this killer new addition to the team, they never did quite find the one zombie that started this whole mess. Whose betrayal cut Claws as deeply as the bite itself on Befana's arm. Their old 'friend' Mortus.

17

HIGHWAY TO HELLO

"**B**ut we'll get him," a pale young man burped into the regretful glare of an older woman as he ended his rant. It had been more than a century now since Claws had announced himself to the world with that shambolic first zombie hunt, though both parties still remained in the periphery of the public's eye—their mythos famous, but existence unconfirmed.

The woman was sitting by the bar in this glorified rathole of a tavern, looking as elegant as she could despite half a bottle of something concerningly just labelled 'AL-COHOL' sloshing around in her stomach. The mature beauty had been wondering whether to call it a night when fate sent her this boozy buck with the definitive answer. Yes, she absolutely should have.

Still, she always *did* have a bit of a thing for the younger gentlemen, and this boyishly charming testosterone factory—*was it Rick*, she mused, *No Nick, he said his name was.* It didn't matter—he looked fresh off the press so why not give him a chance to sweep her off her feet? Unfortunately, as she listened to the inebriating liquids gurgling in the back of his throat, she felt the only action she was likely getting tonight was a projectile vomit straight to the chest. So it seemed highly likely she had just sat through almost an hour of this stranger's life story—or roughly 16 chapters if it were ever novelized—for nothing.

"So, watch out for zombies, they're everywhere. In fact..." Nick continued as he drained another beer glass, his finger pointed squarely at the woman's blurry twin. Had there always been two of them? Perhaps. Then again, he did just mistakenly go to the bathroom in a potted plant nearby—and not a cheeky wee, like you're probably imagining—so he could have just been drunk.

He shook his head to try and undouble his vision but it only worsened the effect. "*You* could be a zombie, and not even know it," the man finished his original thought and casually rested his arm on the bar as the world began to spin. It was funny, here this woman was sitting across from him, probably painting herself as some kind of cougar for entertaining such as young a suitor as him, and yet it was actually *he* that was at least twice *her* age.

After a moment, his vision slowly cleared, and the ghostly twin faded into the smoky haze of a nearby smoker dry-retching 30 years worth of tar out of his lungs. He gazed at the remaining twin with deep-blue eyes that sparkled in the light of a chandelier, and tossed his blond hair to one side—brandishing his boyish charm to conceal the fact that he was totally wasted.

Aside from the disturbing subject matter, the woman found his awkward 'confidence' cute, and it may nearly have worked except for a few minor mood-killers. Like the chandelier that so beautifully brought out his eyes had also been dripping spent candlewax into his last two beers. Or the sweat that had beaded on his forehead due to his never-spoken-to-a-woman-before nerves, now flicked into her face as he tossed the hair that had been clinging to it. And of course, the final straw was the puddle of freshly spilled bar juice now soaking its way up his elbow as it rested obliviously on the bench.

Poor kid.

He deserved points for effort at least—hanging from his stool with reckless exuberance, wobbling like a 25-turn Jenga tower as he spun this crazy story of dragons and monsters to whoever would listen all night. Not that there were many other options around considering how late it was—or early perhaps depending on your intentions—a real Schrodinger's hour of the evening.

"Look," the woman finally stepped in with unfortunately more skepticism than lustful idolization. "When you asked me if you could tell me something, I thought it was just a corny pick-up line to try and get into my pants," she said flatly.

The man paused, "Actually, I was hoping that story would, um..." he babbled, "Is that still an option?"

The woman splashed her drink in his face and stormed off. This brought a smile to the face of a hooded character who had been watching on from the shadows.

"Sorry," he called back. "It's my first time out... never mind," he conceded as he began picking up his coat and readying to leave.

'Twas the night before Christmas, and the few creatures that were still stirring in this particular establishment were doing so crouched in a pool of their own vomit, just putting on the finishing touches before being hosed out the door. But from among the swarm of drunkards, this strapping young barfly was on a mission to find companionship fueled by a classic blend of beer and poor decisions. Strangely enough, his morbid tale of secretly horrifying monsters was not proving the aphrodisiac he had expected, but still, it was sort of his birthday, and his 18-year-old hormones were not ready to pack it in just yet.

Meanwhile, as the midnight sun fell behind the clouds, an ominous gloom engulfed this shithole town, and outside the bar, an old man wandered the snowy streets alone. He stumbled as he walked—possibly homeless, probably drunk—clearly affected by the icy chill hanging in the air despite a brief trail of warmth winding its way down his leg, which snaked a stain of gold through the snow. Right now, he didn't know where, or even who he was, and he certainly had no idea that, a few feet behind him, followed a shadowy figure with the singular focus of ending his night.

There was almost a feral nature to the posture of his pursuer, an intensity in his movement that left no doubt that harm was coming to whoever next he encountered. Like a wolf with its sights on a lost little lamb.

With every stumbling step the wasted walker sheared through the snow, the 'predator' would gain three. As it readied to pounce, the old man suddenly turned, not to catch his attacker off guard, but simply to empty his guts into a nearby drain. The figure crouched down into the cold, pausing to avoid detection. A single stream of drool oozed its way to the ground as its unwavering gaze ensured all focus remained on the target ahead. No sooner did the man finish licking the now-recycled spirits from his lips and turn away, did his pursuer explode into action. Within seconds the pair were united, the attacker growling as he grabbed the old man by the scruff of the neck. He hurled him with manic intensity into a darker doorstep and struck the old man with a wild but effective right hook. He towered over the body ready to finish the job—his hands quivering with anticipation.

The old man was briefly consumed by fear as this creature of the night closed in on its kill. Then as he lay in the cold snow, listening to the sounds of sleigh bells jingling in the distance, he too began to shiver, but more than just from the hypothermic reaction to his approaching death; it was, in fact, some sort of transformation. His eyes rolled back into his head for a moment as a bloodshot glaze possessed them, and his jaws foamed like a rabid mutt. The old man climbed to his feet with veins nearly popping from his arms at the sheer volume of adrenaline hammering through them.

Now, the attacker was the one cowering in fear as he pleaded with the monster to have mercy—though to be fair, he was already tripping balls over some kind of illicit substance he'd snorted earlier, so he could have been talking to a lamp post for all he knew.

The monster rose to defend itself and launched at its now-terrified attacker. A whistling noise cut through the air nearby as it pounced, followed by a sickening wet crack before the creature crashed into the drug addict and the two went tumbling into the street. A lone car nearly ran them over but swerved and blew its horn—about as much effort as anyone here was going to make to intervene. Still screaming from the several recent near-death experiences, the addict grabbed the shoulders of the monster to fend off its attack as he lay pinned beneath it, only to realize it was strangely subdued. He reluctantly pried open his eyes to find himself staring down the headless esophagus of the creature, with the missing piece still smashed into the alley wall where their conflict had begun, and a large red shadow was now disappearing back into the darkness.

"Oh, ho, hooo," came the ghostly echo through the night.

The man hysterically swatted the body away and sprang to his feet. He fumbled a small bag of powder from his pocket and hurled it into a nearby drain. Then shook his head to try and realign his reality. *Did Santa just rescue me from being eaten by a zombie?* he wondered. He had been on some weird trips before, but it must take a really messed up brain to put those two together. *This is the last time I'm getting on that crap again,* he vowed. Of course, he had made that promise once before, after spending three hours arguing with his dinner table. So who knew for sure? Right now, he just needed to get out of there before the rainbow tiger came back.

He ran to a nearby bar, but before he could get in the door, he crashed into the young storyteller who was on his way out. "Whoa, buddy, slow down," said Nick as he patted the panicked addict on the shoulders. "Trust me, you do not want to go in there, it's dead."

The mention of death only served to heighten the man's stress, and he ran in the other direction before disappearing into another bar up the street. *Seems like a good idea*, Nick thought to himself as he rubbed his forehead. It felt like a bunch of hippies were playing hacky sack in there. He needed another drink. It was a strange feeling being out on his own. Spending so long up at the Pole with the old man, he had forgotten what it was like out here.

He wandered over to the next stop on his bar crawl, then stepped cautiously inside and took a long look around the room. What a garbage dump, and the smell matched the appearance, with the broken-down furniture the perfect accompaniment to the scent of stale beer that had long been soaked into the seats. But as he wandered through the dimly lit room searching for some reason to stay, a hen's party drinking its way through a nearby booth lit up like an anglerfish in the Mariana Trench.

Being Christmas time, their conversation had naturally found its way to talk of presents and of course, the big guy. His specialty.

Sensing an opportunity, the young man straightened his shirt and wandered toward them, sitting down at the table with his back to the bar where the half-mangled body of the drug addict was just poking out from behind a keg.

"Ladies," he began confidently. "So you want to know about Santa, hmm? Well, me, I just call him Dad."

18

PLEASED TO MEAT YOU

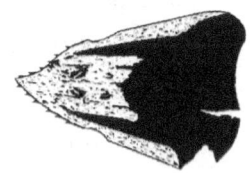

T he young narrator sat perched atop the table in the dingy bar of the shithole town with the four women listening intently as he spoke. If the old saying was to be believed, two may be considered company and three was apparently a crowd. But by this storyteller's reckoning, anything north of that he was penciling in as an orgy, so he was more than keen to see how this night played out.

"Inspired by the old man's heroic deeds," Nick cooed to his prospective bedfellows, "others have secretly taken arms in this battle against the undead, and we now stand guard at the gates of hell holding back this unholy uprising."

The mysterious hooded figure had once again found her way across to the bar for another dose of Nick's exuberant pageantry. This time, her laugh almost drew his attention as she pulled her crimson hood a little lower, though it wasn't long before Nick's audience called him back.

"So, you've actually fought the demons?" asked one of the women, giggling nervously.

"Let's just say they don't call me Saint Nick for nothing," he boasted. No one actually called him that, but he wasn't about to let facts ruin his bedtime story.

"So you're the guy!" she gasped.

"He's not 130," another said doubtfully.

"He looks good for 130," the third admired.

"I do like an older man," the fourth titillated.

Bingo, the young man beamed, congratulating himself.

"Crap," called a drunkard nearby, putting somewhat of a dampener on the increasingly sexual musk that was circling their booth. "Zombies aren't real, and this walking hard-on certainly isn't interested in fighting them." The drunkard snarled as he walked up to one of the women and lifted her skirt with a smile. "But I do know one thing he *is* interested in."

Suddenly Nick, aka *the walking hard-on*, hurled a concealed dragon's tooth, which spun like a ninja star through the air before embedding itself into the flesh of the drunkard's arm. The young woman jumped, partly in objection to the blatant upskirt, and partly from the flying fang striking inches from her head. The drunkard backed away trying to remove the offending enamel as the wound sizzled.

"I figured someone might need convincing," Nick smiled, "Take a look at that ladies: it's a *real* dragon tooth." He frowned as he watched the drunkard's sizzling flesh, studying the phenomenon. "You hear that noise, like meat cooking on a grill?" he instructed the women. "That doesn't happen to most people." Nervous excitement was subtly building in his voice. "Now a zombie on the other hand...," he continued, pulling out a staff and readying to fight.

Suddenly the bartender piped up. He was holding a shotgun, aimed and ready as he wiped a streak of red from his lip. "Off that table and lose the stick or I'll be using it to pick bits o' you outta ma drain. There's no monsters in here."

"Hmmm," Nick mused aloud. "Elevated respiration, unnecessarily aggressive. I say you, sir, are a zombie too." The bartender cocked his gun and began to fire. "Nope, just an arsehole," the youth concluded as he dived out of the way. He swung his staff at a nearby mug like a batter at the perfect pitch, which sent the tin projectile crashing into the bartender's gun, causing him to fire the second round on another patron. Everyone paused as the gunned-down bystander inspected his chest, but as was becoming the theme in this particular corner of hell, instead of falling to his death he rose up as a zombie. The patron jumped onto the bar where the bartender was also making a change of the undead variety himself. The two men grabbed hold of a screaming young gentleman and dragged him behind the bar before the drunkard threw himself into the frenzy as well.

Nick backed away from the bar as the three zombies tore open their gift like a five year old on christmas morning, tossing the fleshy scraps of wrapping paper indiscriminately away as they gorged themselves on the goodies inside. Nick's eyes never left the horror show as he arrived at the table of his female admirers, a look of shock trying to break through his superhero facade. He was a gifted storyteller, no doubt, but perhaps he may have overstated his vast experience with such creatures, which was actually more theoretical in nature than any practical firsthand encounters. The distinct sound of sleigh bells could be heard in the distance as snowflakes mildly seasoned the streets outside.

"Don't worry ladies, I'll protect you," he confidently assured them. To the outside observer his bravado was unquestionable—this guy knew how to handle himself in a fight—but inside he was shaking like a virgin catching his first boob.

Unfortunately, instead of swooning all over their hero, the women swarmed, using far more teeth than tongue—and nobody likes that. *Is everyone in this bar a freaking zombie?*

The hooded woman now slowly rose to her feet amid a rapidly transforming den of beasts, and marched towards the bar as the shot-gunned zombie-patron behind it had finished his meal and now stood, with blood dripping from his jaws, looking for his next victim. As she walked, she slid two daggers from her sleeves and sliced several nearby zombies before they could even react.

The zombie-patron climbed back onto the bar and roared at Nick in a frenzied rage but was cut short by a dagger flying straight through his throat. As blood poured from the wound, he gradually lost balance, then consciousness, and fell back to the floor behind the bar. The woman jumped up to assume his position and dispatched the four floozies with another few flying daggers to the brain. She then looked at the young man and tried her hardest to hide a sneaky smile. "Hey, Nicky. Need a hand?" she chirped.

Nick stood perplexed as he stared at the woman, trying to remember the face. Not many people even knew he existed so it shouldn't have been hard to narrow it down. Her red hooded cape billowed around her as a breeze blew through the bar and her red hair rippled. He'd only ever known one girl to wear such attire. Could this possibly be the young girl from all those years ago in the woods? Surely not. She would have to be over 100 years old as well, but she certainly didn't look it.

As Nick continued to stare, the young woman cleared a few more zombies from his immediate vicinity until the bartender grabbed her by the ankle and latched onto her hooded cape. Her smile instantly vanished in a whirlwind of rage as she ferociously kicked him away. "Don't touch me," she scolded before proceeding to beat the creature senseless as she drove home her message. "And nobody touches the hood!"

Yep, that's definitely her, he concluded.

"Hood," he squeaked, sounding more like a question than a statement. Hood jumped down from the bar with a casualness that belied the threat of the 10 or so zombies surrounding them. "Gates of hell, huh?" she mocked. "Very dramatic."

Nick certainly wasn't sharing her candor as he looked around nervously. Hood followed his gaze and saw an approaching zombie. The change he saw in her demeanor was instantaneous. She stood up and shouted angrily as she kicked it in the chest. Another one vaulted over a table and she threw another dagger across to kill it.

With another spare moment up their sleeve she turned back toward Nick, smiling again. "So, was I really the most beautiful girl you'd ever seen?"

Nick was surprised by the question: he obviously hadn't expected her to hear that part of the story. Or any of it for that matter. *How long has she been following me?* Still, he was kind of glad that she had. "Well, yeah, you were," he agreed. He anticipated a smile or a hug from her, but instead she looked upset.

"Were?" she repeated. "You found someone better looking since then?" Suddenly a zombie grabbed Hood and threw her across the table before Nick could react. He jumped up as he followed her, trying to explain.

"No, I haven't," he babbled defensively while kicking the zombie in the legs. As it fell to the ground, he frantically smashed its head into the table to silence the creature. He wasn't sure which multi-decade reunion was currently scarier, that of the killer zombies that orphaned him, or the orphan zombie killer that wanted him. He was on some kind of rollercoaster at the moment, and he didn't know whether he wanted to scream or sing or throw up or pass out.

"Oh, but you've looked," Hood continued. She went to grab another dagger from her belt, but was all out, so she simply tossed the next zombie back up over the bar.

Nick took another step closer to where Hood was fending off another. "Well, I mean, I'm a young guy I guess, relatively speaking, and I didn't even know you felt the same way," he continued apologetically before frustration also drew him to question her. "Also, how are you even still alive?"

"I dunno, same as you, I guess," she replied, not being overly helpful. "How did *you* do it?"

"It's a long story," Nick shook his head dismissively, overwhelmed by the commotion, "I don't really have time to get into it right now."

"Oh, I see, so you mean I've searched for you all this time," Hood ripped one of her daggers out of a previous kill and began stabbing the nearest zombie ferociously, "and you haven't even given me a second thought?"

Nick was quite stunned. "No, I mean yes, of course I have..." Hood kicked the zombie back into another pile and ran back over to look Nick in the eyes. He flinched, not surprisingly given the rage he'd just witnessed her unleash on the zombies.

"Relax, Nicky, I'm messing with you," she smiled again. "I know you want me." And damn it if she wasn't right.

Suddenly the drunkard rose up from the bar chuckling. His speech was even more slurred, suggesting that he may have paired the human flesh he was feasting on back there with a bottle of soft and fruity merlot. "Sho maybe you're tellin the truth. Not about the zombiesh, well..." He looked down at the blood all over himself and half shrugged in acceptance as he stumbled, "maybe that too, but about the other guy, Santa." There was a real sense of displeasure in saying the name.

"You tell that roly-poly pretty boy that he better shtay away from here. The King hatesh him," he said as Nick looked at him with confusion on his face.

"King? As in, like one of you?" asked Nick, trying to understand how such a thing would even be possible.

"Not like me. Your dad changed him, made him stronger. He's got big plans for this town," the drunk rambled.

"Morty," Nick whispered.

"A Zombie King is coming here?" Hood growled.

The drunk realized he had said too much so he doubled down with his threat since there was no point hiding anything now. His accelerated metabolism was burning through the alcohol faster than the average person, so he was sobering up already.

"You can stick around if you want but you're gonna die. You all will," he sneered.

"Good enough for me," smiled Hood, immune to the threats being tossed around as she gathered up her daggers from the corpses strewn across the bar.

"Where are you going?" Nick called to her—just as a friend looking out for another friend. At least that's the platonic, nice-guy angle he was going to start with until she was ready to marry him. "In case I need to contact you or give you something," he babbled. And boy did he want to give her something.

She didn't look convinced.

"Maybe I could even come with you?" he pleaded. Nick was getting desperate to ensure another meeting.

Outside the bar a silhouette passed by the window and a familiar cough 'Ho, ho'd' its way through the cracks in the walls.

"I work alone remember?" she smiled as she walked to the door. "I've gotta see this King for myself. And then kill him, of course. I love a challenge." Loving and exciting as her smile was, every now and then Nick got this psychopathic vibe from it as well. *Everyone's a little crazy, right?* he mused. She just had a little higher dose than anyone else he'd ever met.

Hood turned toward the door just as a big black boot kicked it down. "Looks like someone's been naughty…" a sinister voice began amid a smoke cloud, but as Claws stepped through the doorway Hood cut him off.

"Too slow, old man. I left one for you, though," she muttered monotonously with a sigh as she clipped his shoulder with hers and exited the bar.

Claws slumped in disappointment as he surveyed the room. It took him years to get up the confidence to pull that catchphrase back out of the bag after his disastrous first hunt, and he really wanted to make an entrance with his kid now officially watching. Once again, it was ruined. His look turned to confusion as he looked back at the girl. "Red Riding Hood?" he recalled.

"It's just Hood," she replied impatiently. Then in a blink she was gone.

Claws called back out through the door at the empty alley way. "You may think you're being cool with that whole grim and despair routine, but it sucks to be alone. Trust me. My offer still stands, there's a home here if you want it." No reply.

Above them on the roof, Hood was sitting quietly. Listening. Thinking.

Claws turned and assessed Nick to make sure he was all right until Nick sheepishly nodded all clear. Claws then turned toward the drunkard and walked toward him as Nick filled him in. "I know I've got a lecture coming, and you probably want to kill this guy to get started but you might want to hold off for a second. I think he knows something about You Know Who."

Claws pushed the drunkard back into a chair. He leaned down close and stared him down. "Interesting," he smiled devilishly.

"Do tell."

19

CLAWSTROPHOBIC

A few nights later Claws stroked his great white beard thoughtfully as he sat by the fire at the North Pole. He was browsing some maps while Ralph slept soundly at his feet. The young dragon was now the size of a large moose—his growth rate slowing with age—and his furry hide was beginning to make way for much tougher scales. His breath still flickered with flames, and it seemed more likely now a defect in his respiratory system than a mere muscle he would learn to control. But aside from a few singed hairs or burnt clothing here and there, the family had made peace with it as just part of who he was. Plus, he doubled as a handy nightlight.

After a moment, Claws rattled the chain of claws around his neck as he considered the words of the drunken monster at the bar. It had told him that Mortus was hiding in the very town where Claws first hunted Nick's zombie family.

He had heard such whispers and whereabouts before from victims or minions of this self-proclaimed Zombie King—and they were always false or far too late for Claws to catch him. But this one felt different, it was almost as if it were offered as a challenge, confident to the point of arrogance rather than seemingly the feeble gasp of a monster drowning in its own blood. Perhaps Morty was getting cocky in his old age, if somehow, he was even still alive. Or *perhaps it's a trap*, he mused.

His mind wandered back to the day Befana was attacked, and the rhythmic rattle of the necklace helped stir his raging soul to action. He smiled and rose from his chair.

"Befana!" he bellowed authoritatively. "Grab my coat. I'm going out!"

Befana wandered in washing her hands—clearly not sharing the level of enthusiasm her husband was experiencing. She looked good. Her long-term exposure to the dragons and Claws was improving her condition and lending a more permanent glow to her skin. As she tapped her fingertips together, she could still feel her nerves tingling almost an hour after her last contact with Claws. She may never be rid of her unchained alter ego, but still, her body was healing. She was smiling and looked at her husband with a serving of skepticism laced with an undeniable hint of curiosity.

"And what have you found this time? Is the Bunny on another rampage through the streets?"

"You know damn well that abomination can't be trusted!" said Claws, instantly outraged. "He tricks children into eating his sweet poisonous droppings and kidnaps them."

"You're just mad because you ate some," she mocked.

"It's called an addiction, darling! I love my sweets and I thought they were chocolate eggs."

Befana laughed at her husband's stupidity. "Birds lay eggs, fish lay eggs. If something round comes out of a rabbit, I'd be thinking twice before putting it in my mouth."

"You think twice before putting anything in your mouth," he mumbled under his breath.

"Excuse me!" she exclaimed with her shocked expression drawing panic from the great slayer.

"Nothing, I'm just hangry now, that's all," he complained.

"Oh, you poor dear. Should I go see if the dragons have left any chocolate in the barn?" Befana laughed again.

Claws sighed in defeat "One handful, I ate one handful of that creature's delicious excrement, and you'll never let me live it down. Besides, it's not about the damn Bunny, it's the wrong time of year. I think I've found *HIM*."

Befana's smile evaporated. "Oh Claws, not this again. It's been years since anyone's even heard from him, and I know you made a promise, but I can't keep getting my hopes up every time some monster starts limping or Ralph picks up a scent."

At the sound of his name, Ralph's head bolted to attention.

"About you, honey, not to you," Befana cooed as she patted him back down to sleep.

Claws tossed his map to the ground stubbornly. "I know that sweetheart, but I can't just ignore it. Even if there's only a chance it's him, I'll take it, and if not, I've rid the world of a few more of those creatures, at least. Besides, I've been wanting to take young Nick out on his first hunt for years now. It'll be good to show him what the old man does for a living. He might like it."

"He saw firsthand what you do for a living the night you killed all his family, remember?" she shot back. "And I'll never forgive you for leaving him there alone. Who knows what could have happened to him that night?"

"We've been through this a hundred times. I thought he would be a lot safer *after* my visit than before it. And I did go back for him, didn't I?"

"Only after I told you that house would look like Candy Land compared to what I was going to do to you if you didn't," she snapped back. "And it still took you a month!"

"I'm a busy man darling." Claws smiled to himself, taking a more pleasant tangent from the current conversation. "Ah, I still remember him that night. He was so excited to get in that kitchen and see what I had left for him downstairs, he must have told everyone about the great man in red who had come to visit him," Claws chuckled nostalgically. "The look on his face would have been priceless if anyone would have let him in there."

He laughed to himself but Befana was unimpressed. She pulled the pin on a disapproving remark and readied to toss it like a live grenade in Claws' direction.

"The point is he came back eventually," interrupted a voice from the hallway. "I decided to tag along, the bad guys got what they deserved, and we all lived happily ever after. Now can we go?" said Nick, the young man from the bar, as he stood in the doorway. Despite sporting that deathly white glow courtesy of years living at the Pole, he was quite handsome and strong like his father—though he was more toned and slender than the fatty bulk his old man now carried around.

He was impatient to get out, and tried to hurry them along. "Besides, I got a pretty good idea the other night when..." He paused at the sight of his father signaling for him to kill the conversation until Befana spotted their silent code.

"You took him with you?" she glared at Claws. "You told me he wasn't ready. *I* told you he wasn't ready."

"And you were right, again," Claws shrugged defensively, "so you can go ahead and stick that one on your resume." The old couple bickered furiously but not altogether aggressively.

"Oh, I know where I'll be sticking it," she barked, the slightest hint of red creeping into her eyes. This was Claws' cue to cool things off and gave a cheeky grin to defuse the situation as he turned his backside in her direction ready to welcome her.

"Oh, it's always about sex with you, isn't it? All right then, have at me," grinned Claws. Befana's serious tone was now being undermined by a sneaky smile creeping up her lip. Damn her husband's charms.

"You guys are disgusting," Nick stood nearby looking unimpressed. Claws laughed at both the stupidity of the conversation and his son's reaction to it. Befana still smiled a little but her embarrassment overpowered the joy. She started to get upset again.

"You know I didn't want you to take him. Why don't you ever listen?" she pleaded.

Claws could see the time for jokes had passed. "Look I needed a scout with a fresh face, and he wouldn't take no for an answer," he said as he walked up and looked her in the eye. This was his slam-dunk, end-of-conversation finisher, because as soon as she got a puff of his breath in her lungs, the endorphins flooding her system turned her to putty in his hands. She couldn't resist. "You have done absolutely everything you can to prepare him for this world, now we just have to push him out of the nest and he'll either spread his wings and fly or break every bone in his body when he nosedives into the dirt.'

"Thanks, Dad," Nick smirked sarcastically. Claws just smiled and put his finger to his lips as Befana began to chuckle. She knew exactly what he was doing. He pulled out this move whenever he got desperate in an argument to try and soften her up. This was her victory, when she knew he was stumped, and it came with the added bonus of an endorphin kick. "Besides," Claws continued, "he didn't do anything anyway. I dragged him out at the first sign of trouble. Not even a scratch."

"Yeah, what was that all about? I had it covered. Don't tell me you're going to let me go, and then take over before I get a chance to kill anything," said Nick, pouting like a child.

"Now, don't you start. I'm not going to just throw you in the deep end and hope for the best," said Claws. "You dipped your toe in, got a feel for it. Now you might not be so terrified the next time you come face to face with a zombie."

Nick opened his mouth to argue but felt the job had already been done in convincing Befana of his safety. Besides it wasn't a total lie. It did take him by surprise when he saw the zombies up close and he had been pretty glad when someone stepped in. It just wasn't Claws that did the saving. Luckily, his mother interrupted before he had to take the lie any further.

"All right, all right, take him. But you two be careful out there. If you run into any trouble, I'll know about it," Befana could hear herself nagging the boys and stopped.

"You could come too, you know, Mom," said Nick. "I've never seen you in a proper fight, but Dad says you're heaps better than he is."

Claws defensively chimed in to object. "I may have mentioned that she had some skills back in the day, but there's not a soul on this planet that can best your old man." Befana smiled as Claws continued, "I may have talked you up from time to time but I never said you were better than me. That's crazy!"

Befana walked over to her son and hugged him. "That's a very nice offer but I decided a long time ago to let your father handle the rough stuff. I'm happy helping in a less... stressful capacity. It's just easier this way."

The boys walked off to get ready, and Nick leaned over to his father. "But I thought you said she was better than you."

"Never mind what I said, you can't go telling *her* that." Claws lightheartedly lectured. "I have to live with her you know."

Befana could still hear them. She just smiled and waved them off as they headed to the stable. Ralph nudged past her to join them.

"And thanks for covering for me there," Nick smiled at his old man.

"Oh, please, I was young once. I couldn't wait to get out on my own and find an adventure, and I didn't have to wait nearly as long as you. Just let me know next time you're going to do it. It never hurts to have some back-up. Though I saw you already had that covered," said Claws as he tousled Nick's hair playfully. Nick had just spent half an hour getting it just right, so he wasn't impressed, but he managed a chuckle anyway for the sake of his dad.

"And what about you and Red Riding Hood, huh?" Claws interrogated him with a smile.

"Her name is Hood," Nick surprised himself with how defensive he sounded.

"Oh sorry, I don't want to offend the girlfriend." Claws apologized. "Do we need to have... the talk?" Claws worked hard to squeeze out those uncomfortable few words like the pasty dregs from an empty tube of toothpaste.

"Dad, I'm an 18-year-old man with a computer. Trust me, I know everything I could ever want to."

Claws sighed heavily, thanking any deity that was listening for that reprieve. Although, realistically, his son was more than a century old, his body was only just getting started in that crazy testosterone-fueled time of life. Claws was breaking out in a sweat just thinking about having that discussion. He patted Nick on the leg and stared at the floor. "Well, good, that's good," he mumbled awkwardly.

Age was a relative figure in this household. By now they had worked out that the dragon breath slowed the aging process to about 10 percent of the average human rate, and muscle decay also occurred far slower as well, meaning mobility and power remained despite the increase in age. So, for every actual birthday Claws celebrated, a regular person would see 10. Kind of like calculating dog years, only it's the human that ages faster.

For Claws, this meant that, even though he was currently pushing almost 200 in human years, he still possessed the silver fox charm of a man in his 50s if you took into account the first 35 years of his life—pre-dragon breath—were spent aging at a regular pace. And he still felt as strong as he ever had.

Claws tried not to think about the Maths behind it too much. It gave him a headache.

Now in the case of young Nick, Claws picked him up already aged five and a half, and it wasn't long before Ralph gave him a blast of that special gas during a playful tussle in the weeks following his arrival at the Pole. So he then spent the next 125 years of his life living there at the adjusted rate of maturity, content in his bubble, safe from harm, and protected by his parents. Now immortality is great, but at that rate, it took him 50 years just to hit puberty, and by his 130th year on this Earth he was finally able to celebrate his '18th birthday' with that sneaky trip to the bar. And, boy, did he need a drink. Anyone who tells you childhood is the best years of your life, try giving them 13 decades to endure and see how quickly they change their tune.

Obviously by this stage Nick was quite an intelligent guy and a very skillful fighter, after all, there wasn't much else for he and his mother to do there but read and train since neither really left the village all that often.

Every now and then Claws would sneak him out on a hunt to wait in the sleigh while he took care of business. It was a bit of a treat for them both, and a chance for the young man to experience the world beyond the burg. Befana was more worried about life outside than Claws was, which made sense given what she had been through herself.

For some added protection, Claws would leave Larry in charge to watch over the boy and keep him out of trouble. But, of course, Larry didn't really care what the kid did, and would simply follow behind to study him when he snuck away to explore. Claws knew what was going on. When Nick was younger, sometimes Claws would come back to the sleigh, and the pair would not yet have returned from their spying, so he would pretend to still be away fighting and wait for Nick to sneakily crawl back into the sleigh. When Claws finally "returned" Nick would always pretend to be asleep with a cheeky grin plastered across his face. Other times he would catch a glimpse of the young boy hiding somewhere safely, watching him hack apart some horrifying creature. It gave him a certain sense of pride knowing his son was watching, learning, and admiring his work.

He may not have liked the idea of Nick being away from the sleigh and vulnerable, but he knew the time was coming when hormones and curiosity would drive him to wander anyway, and preferred it to happen under the watchful eye of that mini tornado than have Nick sneaking out alone. Larry may have been standoffish, condescending and quite possibly homicidal, but he was also fiercely loyal as well, and Claws trusted him implicitly, especially since he had saved Larry's life against the witch. That really earned him some brownie points.

Nick's escape to the bar was a surprise for Claws in more ways than one. He had been holding onto this dream that his little boy would stay safe at home forever, not realizing he had already left years ago, replaced by a man ready to step out on his own and make his mark on the world. It was time.

20

COMIN' TO TOWN

Very early the next morning—or very late the night before it—in the hours before the sun had even dragged its lazy ass out of bed, the two men loaded up the sleigh and said their final goodbyes. Then the dragons took off. They were all much older and larger now—though Ralph was still the biggest—and were strong enough to pull them straight up into the air. They were also all quite capable fire-breathers, despite Ralph's defect giving him limited control. Sometimes it worked, sometimes it didn't. Befana often joked about that particular similarity between her husband and his dragon, so Claws could certainly empathize with his performance issues.

The dark elves created an exit through the ice with their coal pellets in a well-worn routine. Nick sat starry eyed at the front, his mind lost in a tug-of-war between nervous paralysis and adrenaline-fueled exuberance. But this time the adrenaline was winning. His last adventure had done him some good. This time he knew what was coming and was ready to go. Adding to that was thoughts of Hood. He knew she'd be lurking around somewhere in that town—probably fighting something far bigger or more powerful than she was. That was kind of her thing, but if she hadn't already got herself killed yet, Nick was looking forward to running into her at some stage of the morning.

As they neared the town, Claws began to gather his blood-red jacket—the color had grown on him—and flail from the back of the sleigh while Nick pulled out a long wooden staff with small blades embedded in it up and down its length. The middle third was vacant, instead coated in a tar-like grip. He swung it above his head for some practice, prompting a curious inspection from his father.

"What is that?" Claws frowned as he stared at the staff.

"I've been collecting all the baby teeth the dragons lost growing up," said Nick. "I tried using one the other night in the bar, which was pretty effective, so I thought I'd test a theory."

Just then the dragons seemed to get agitated and began to speed up. Claws could sense something as well. "I'm getting a really strong feeling from this town," he noted. "It's like nothing I've felt before. He must be here."

Claws shook his head and took a more serious tone of conversation. "OK, we're passing over our entry point now. Big house, small family, Mom and Dad are already too far gone. Let's lay down some ground rules. This is your first official hunt so let's keep things as simple as possible.

Firstly, don't get bitten. We got lucky the other night, but I don't know how you'll respond, and I don't want to test it. Second, stay behind me and follow my lead. Take it moment by moment, one by one—it's easy to get overwhelmed. Thirdly, trust no one but the people up here on, or pulling, this sleigh. And lastly, if you see the one that turned your mother, leave him for me. We've got some catching up to do before I let him leave this world."

"Oh, and try and keep quiet," Claws added. "The success of this job is when people don't know we've been until we've already left."

"Discretion, got it," said Nick as he jumped over the side of the sleigh down toward the roof of a two-story house. They were still quite some distance in the air, but his excitement fueled his charge.

Claws sighed and signaled for some of the dark elves to follow.

Larry had no interest in jumping down there, but with Pete standing absent-mindedly to his right, it took only a simple push for the other elf to 'volunteer.' Now Larry would never admit to harboring such base primitive urges as anger or grudge-holding, but there was a certain level of satisfaction in knocking the clueless minion into the darkness. *So long Zwarte-Piet,* Larry chuckled to himself as he settled back into his seat.

Surprised as he was, Pete set straight to work, raining down coal at the rooftop as he fell. The coal crashed into the faded tiles just seconds before Nick did, and the young hunter went straight through the freshly blackened break-point as if tearing through paper. He hit the family lounge at speed, and the room exploded with poultry feathers.

The husband and wife wandered nervously from their rooms to inspect the commotion. As the air cleared their attacker was revealed, standing confidently on the near unrecognizable pile of fabric that was once their sofa.

"So," the athletic intruder taunted as a fractured shin-bone sucked back into his leg. "Hands up if you're a zombie."

Suddenly a young boy wandered out from his bedroom rubbing his eyes and hugged his father's leg as the family held one another closer. "Santa?" quizzed the boy innocently, he looked six years old at most.

Nick was frozen in place as he stared at the young boy. Memories flooded back to the crippling aftermath of his own family's demise, which he was forced to endure at that same tender age. He could only imagine what horrors were to come for this orphan-to-be once he'd finished the job. He glanced back up to the hole in the roof. Maybe it wasn't too late to get out of here. Maybe they were great parents after all, even if they were zombies.

He didn't have long to stew on his cowardice because the father attacked with a rabid flash of teeth to wrench him from his thoughts. Nick stumbled back to dodge the dad, before receiving a solid punch to the jaw from the wife while the man vaulted off a nearby wall to kick Nick in the chest. Nick tripped over a chair as he crashed to the floor and scrambled backward to pull himself up on a wall. He swung his staff wildly in his panic until the father grabbed it—though only briefly as it burned in his hand, forcing him to let go. The young hunter's mind was spinning; everything was going so fast as he struggled to fend off their attacks.

Nick knew he was the better fighter. He knew he could wipe the floor with them if he wanted, but every time he looked at these parents protecting their young, he couldn't help but remember his own and wonder if maybe this wasn't the best thing for the kid. Maybe he should just leave. Maybe they were awesome zombie parents. Nick wore several more shots as he stumbled through the house, the battle more in his own mind really than the battered living room.

Again Nick was effortlessly tossed and crashed against the wall. The parents stood waiting a moment, as if to see whether the young man was ready to surrender. Then behind the parents Nick could make out the figure of the young boy running toward him. He saw the child leap through the air, with perhaps a hint of crazy in his eye, but at the last second Nick instinctively caught and hurled the young boy to the side, sending him smashing through a nearby cupboard door.

The boy did not come back out. Nick was horrified. Did he just kill a kid? *What if the boy had just been defending his parents? What have I done?* His mind raced with questions. A shot of adrenaline surged through his body as he struck both parents aside and ran toward the cupboard to check on the kid. Inside, he saw the boy crouched down in a pile of random body parts, gnawing on what appeared to be a rib. He had never been so relieved and disgusted in a single moment, and as a mouthful of vomit swirled around his tongue, his head finally cleared, and he was ready to retaliate.

"Hey, kid," he smirked casually as the child raised its feral head, "Thanks, and call me Nick.' The kid obviously didn't care who he was or how he had assisted him, but now Nick knew his enemy, and had indeed learned the value of Claws' third rule.

With his confidence restored, Nick turned back toward the parents who were charging at him again. He spun his staff as he walked between them, striking them as they passed. Each cut sizzled as the teeth broke the skin, and they staggered to the opposite side of the room to regroup. The husband grabbed an axe from next to the fireplace and swung it wildly, but Nick blocked each shot with relative ease.

The man raised the axe above him and brought it down as if to split Nick's head like a log of wood, but with an inch to spare, Nick caught the axe on the center of his staff. After taking a second to assess, he noticed the wife running up behind him, and the son exiting the cupboard with a razor-sharp bone clutched in his hand.

Nick spun his staff to dislodge the axe from the husband's grasp, while striking and kicking him back. He then snatched the falling axe from the air as the man stumbled backward, and threw it at the rabid zombie child to behead it. Next was the mother's turn, and Nick was not about to waste a moment on her. He pressed a button on his staff which shot a corded knife straight through the throat of the approaching woman, and no sooner did it split her spine in two did he rip the cord back through along with several inches of esophagus. Though he was quick and deliberate in his actions and clearly well trained, there was still a sense of madness to his method. You would almost call it a panic as he battled his own nerves, finally putting those long hours of practice into real life action.

Finally, two quick slashes of his razor-sharp staff beheaded the husband before his spouse's corpse had a chance to even hit the ground. The second of those slashes really had some heat on it as he burned the last of that nervous energy to send the skull flying like a batter latching on to a pitch.

The head sailed through the air toward an open window. Nick held his breath as he waited for it to fly out into the street and be discovered, but as it neared the window a dark coal pellet struck the homeless head, and it disappeared in a dusty cloud as it passed out into the night air. Nick looked up to see Larry watching over him and smiled as he began to relax.

It was all over within minutes, and Nick breathed a sigh of relief as he observed the mayhem. Not bad for a first timer. Soon the bulkier frame of his father swung down through the roof and landed heavily on the ground. Some of the dragons peered down through the hole as the dark elves began patching it up. Claws looked around the room and nodded his approval.

"Clean, quiet and relatively quick. That's the dream tri-fecta," his father admired as he wandered over to shut the window. He didn't say anything about the near slip-up, but it was his subtle way of letting the boy know that he saw it, and more care must be taken. "We might actually get out of here tonight without the whole town hearing us. Now let's go dig up that scumbag, I'm still sensing a lot of zombies in this town and he could be anywhere."

"Getting warmer..." a sinister voice echoed from below. Claws and Nick shared a concerned look.

The voice taunted again, "You in there, buddy?" The word 'buddy' was spat with such venom that Claws was cautious in his approach. He leaned out the window to see a cloaked figure standing in the central square of the town, dimly lit by streetlamps, but enough to get a look at him. The figure calmly raised his arms to remove his hood and revealed himself to be Mortus, the monster who had turned Befana all those years ago. The years had not been kind to him. Without the constant exposure to the dragon breath's healing power—as Claws and his family had enjoyed—his body looked broken from years of abuse and he looked like a man pushing 70, though that could also be taken as a compliment considering how old he actually was. Maybe it was the virus or perhaps something else, but despite his age he still looked as powerful as the day he first locked horns with Claws.

"It's been quite a while, old friend," he sneered, as he held up the claw chain around his neck and smiled mockingly. "How's the wife?"

Claws took a step to jump out the window, but Nick held him back. "Dad, wait."

Then with ominous synchronicity, every door on every house began to open and the townsfolk wandered slowly into the street. Claws yelled down to them. "Get back in your homes. That man is a monster. He's going to kill you." But no-one even reacted to his call. It was a trap.

"Oh, I wouldn't worry so much about them if I were you," the cloaked figure responded forebodingly before raising a hand to the crowd and pointing at Claws. "This is the man who has come to destroy you," he bellowed.

Suddenly Claws noticed the hundreds of bystanders begin to transform into the monstrous creatures he'd hunted for years. As far back as the town stretched, he could see more appearing, and Nick quickly ran to the other side of the house to see hundreds more over there. This crowd was certainly bigger than anything Claws had ever faced, and he struggled to comprehend how to even begin taking them out.

But what baffled him most was the level of organization at play here. To coordinate this mindless horde into an undead army, that's not something he would have thought their disease-hampered intellects would be capable of fathoming.

He turned his attention back to the rather smugly smiling Mortus. "How are you doing this, Mortus? How are you even still alive? We're almost 200 years old, you should be nothing but compost by now."

"The human mind is a beautiful thing, Claws. So delicate by design, yet powerful and unyielding even to the most horrifying of attacks. This affliction of mine has given me unimaginable power and you, I must admit, have given me the means to control it—and them if I just push the right buttons," said Mortus, as he motioned to the crowd. "One breath we shared in battle a lifetime ago may not have healed these old bones completely," he lifted his pants leg to show a twisted, scarred leg and pointed to another scar across his face. "But it does seem to have slowed my aging considerably. Not that I should give you much credit for my survival. You may have been gifted an easy passage through life with that immortal flame bubbling away in your chest, but I've had to scrap and fight for every birthday. I have killed so many, of my kind and yours, to get myself here, waiting for this day. And now here we are."

Suddenly there was a commotion on the roof. The dragons were getting restless. Claws signaled for Nick to go check it out as he leaned out the window to his long-lost nemesis. "So, what's the plan, Morty? I pushed you around, made you feel weak, so you murder a town full of people to prove me wrong. You're a coward. Always have been. You want me, come fight me like a man."

"The time for you giving orders has long passed its expiry," replied Mortus. "This town has been liberated and they are just the beginning! I am no longer your slave but a king, and I'm building an army to formalize my rule. They are stronger and faster than any military force on the planet, without pain or fear of death. Better yet, they are perfectly at ease with complete subjugation to me. Of course, your dragons offer that final ingredient to make them truly invincible. With the healing power those winged wonders possess, no one can stop us. Not even you."

Suddenly Nick smashed down through a new hole in the roof. He had some blood on him but luckily it wasn't his. He was breathing heavily, clearly from a fight. "Dad, the dragons..." he began before they saw within the zombie horde a netted dragon being dragged toward the outspoken aggressor.

"He was just drawing our attention for an ambush," Nick said breathlessly. "They've got Ralph."

"Ah just in time, I was starting to run out of monologue," said Mortus. "Thanks for so predictably bringing me your little pets. Well, this one in particular actually. You always were such a dumb giant. That's why it burned me so much to see you succeed on sheer brute force while my superior intellect languished in anonymity. Well, those wrongs are about to be set right. Consider this your retirement party, old man.

Santa Claws is dead!"

21

VIOLENT NIGHT

Mortus, the Zombie King, signaled for his army to move in, and the undead swarm began its march toward the house. "Protect yourselves, my friends. Kill the invader!" he ordered, then to Claws he sneered with utter contempt, "See you soon, boss."

Nick wandered over to Claws and whispered in his ear. "Dad, there must be a thousand of them. What are we gonna do?"

Claws looked up through the hole in the roof at the dark elves who were awaiting his orders. "Tell the other dragons to get out of here. Then you three lay down some cover-fire from up there. Take as many of them out as you can." The elves disappeared and suddenly the dragons began flying around the house breathing fire on the rabid townsfolk. Claws grabbed Nick and dragged him to the staircase. "I don't know how this is going to go down but if you keep your head and remember what I taught you there's a good chance we'll get through this. I won't let anything happen to you."

Nick's eyes looked glassy. "I wish Mom was here," he whispered, trying to hold back the tears. He was scared.

"Good talk son," snapped Claws. "Thanks for the shot of confidence." He was irritated by Nick's lack of faith in him but, in truth, he was worried himself. There was no sense putting Nick down. If they were to have any chance of escaping here they needed to be a team. They needed to be strong and work together.

"OK," Claws put a hand on Nick's shoulder and looked him in the eye. "The truth is I can't see a way out. And there's a good chance we won't walk away from this house. And maybe we could have used Mom's help, but I don't want her stuck in this mess anymore than I want you to be. So here we are. Now as large and as terrifying as that army may seem, it does have an end, and for every zombie you kill, that end gets closer. You know you can beat one, right? Just beat that one guy a thousand times. Then we save Ralph and get out of here."

Nick smiled. As scared as he was with the threat of annihilation bearing down on them, his dad had a way of making it all seem bearable. The truth was he did wish his mother was there. They probably couldn't win this alone. But if he was going to go down swinging, no one swung harder than his old man, and as long as he was breathing, he knew they had a chance.

"Oh, and be careful son, your mother and I, we…" Claws struggled to finish his sentence. The L-word caught in the tough guy's throat like a poisonous rabbit shit.

"I know Dad," said Nick, who knew Claws was never great at this emotional crap, so he gave his dad a hand. "I love you too… So, what's the plan?"

Claws sighed with relief then drew a breath. Time to go to work. "I'll take the front door; you take the back. Fall back to the stairs if it all gets too much." He grabbed a flail in each hand and charged down the stairs. Nick twisted his staff to expose two knives tipped with dragon blood sticking out either end. He took a deep breath and charged down after his father.

No sooner did they reach their posts than the creatures arrived at the door. Claws jammed a chair against the handle of the front door and swung through the window onto the porch. The first creature was already banging on the door as he swung the flail into the back of its head to kill it. "One," he counted quietly to himself. He then dispatched a few more before looking out over the mass of zombies heading his way.

The sun was just starting to leak a little color into the blackened sky, and he could see the dragons swooping and breathing flames on their attackers in the distance. Meanwhile dark pellets rained down from the roof hitting arms, legs, chests, and dropping limbs and bodies in rapid succession—though the sheer volume of their enemy meant a dent in their number was barely made. *It's a shame*, he thought as he looked out at the old crappy buildings behind the army, *I always liked this town*. The modern technological age was spreading faster than this monstrous disease, yet this little spot remained anchored in the past, a testament to the old world, like him.

As the rest of the army drew nearer, Claws stomped on one end of a wooden step, which popped the other end up into his hand. He javelined the now-broken wood into the chest of an approaching zombie then retreated back inside the window to wait.

Over on Nick's side of the house, he took a more direct approach. As he neared the door, one of the zombies was pushing it open, and Nick powerfully kicked the wood so hard that it slammed shut on the zombie and flew off its hinge back through the doorframe. The door pushed all those who were following it back out onto the street.

He stood atop the door with the crushed zombie underneath and took in the mass of creatures now charging toward him. "One," he counted quietly to himself.

He leaped into the crowd, spinning his staff and slicing the zombies to pieces. His weapon sizzled as it swung through them like fresh meat on a hotplate, and though they swarmed around him, none could get through the rapidly spinning bladed staff.

He grew comfortable for a moment as he danced among them, lulled into security by their utter capitulation to his blade. Then he noticed the group parting several rows back and the gap was drawing nearer. When it reached the front, he saw a gigantic, strong man launch himself from the crowd towards Nick. The rookie caught a flash of red as he dived to the side, narrowly missing the attacker, and was immediately set upon by three creatures. As he lay on his back, he held them at bay with his staff while their salivating daemon mouths bore down on him. He shook his staff from side to side, cutting them more and more until they released, giving him precious seconds to retreat.

The giant man then returned and threw a powerful punch, which Nick blocked and stumbled backward. The dragons' teeth burned on the giant's massive arm, but it simply snarled and continued to attack. As Nick blocked and parried, the giant's skin continued to burn, but even a blocked punch from this mammoth man still jarred his arms and pushed him backwards. Each strike it *did* land through Nick's defenses gave the creature greater impetus to go on, and its attack became wild and frenzied. The smell was becoming quite overwhelming as more burning zombie flesh was exposed. Then the giant creature grabbed Nick's staff. A brief tug-of-war ensued before it began swinging him around when he refused to let go. He was knocking zombies over left and right as he flapped like a fish on the end of the staff.

Eventually his grip failed under the force of the swing, and he shattered a window as he sailed back into the house. Some of the creatures tried to rush inside to follow as Nick climbed painfully to his feet. He saw them run into the doorway and waited for them to streak through the other side but, instead, they just fell down dead through the doorway—one, two, three—each with a tiny dagger poking out of the back of their heads. Nick smiled as he waited for the next person to step through the doorway. Hood!

"Hey, Nicky, need a hand? Wait, have we done this before?" she asked as she reached down to help him up.

Claws stood with his back to the door. When the first zombie poked its head through the window, Claws bashed it with a quick strike of his flail, knocking it back outside. Another then copied the action and received a duplicate punishment for its troubles. Soon the window on the other side of the door smashed and Claws used the second flail to bop any heads that dared look in over there, playing Whack-a-Mole with zombie heads.

Suddenly, he felt a larger bump on the door. "Who is it?" he called, knowing full well his chances of a normal response were slim to none.

A deep, evil-sounding "Baaaa" was the unnerving response before two flaming zombie sheep jumped through the windows and circled him like sharks.

"What the hell?" he cried as the sheep charged sporadically in his direction, and though they were quick, their kamikaze fighting style was not the most accurate form of attack. He dodged their lunges as he threw himself from side to side, still trying to digest the nature of this new threat. They were clumsy in their movements and continually slipped or crashed into the walls and furniture. The curtains inevitably caught fire, which seemed to keep the other zombies from following them through the window for now.

Soon the flames and livestock barrage forced him to leave his post at the door. The sheep chased him through the hallway at maddening speeds, and he leaped up to grab a chandelier to dodge one charging through beneath him. As they disappeared into the surrounding maze of rooms, he could still hear the soulless beat of their hooves clattering along the floorboards and getting louder as they made their way back for another run. Claws searched for somewhere to go and spotted a cupboard. He opened the door and was about to jump inside when suddenly he had an idea. As the sheep came around again, Claws stood next to the cupboard with the door closed once more, and waited as if he had all the time in the world. Sensing an easy kill, the woolly wildfires upped their pace but just as they were about to hit him, he opened the cupboard door again. They crashed into it hard, and Claws did his best to absorb the impact by propping his shoulder against the other side to save it ripping off its hinges. He then slammed the door shut with the two sheep forced inside.

"Yeah, yeah," Nick grinned sheepishly at Hood as he climbed back out through the window on the other side of the house. "Just watch the door for me would you? I think I dropped something out here." He really wanted to prove to Claws he could hold his end and was not about to retreat.

Hood followed her orders and stood guard at the doorway, slicing and skewering any zombie that came within arm's reach of the interior. Meanwhile, Nick waited patiently for the giant creature to return with his staff. He was ready this time. The creature held it by one end, its hand still sizzling as the blades cut its skin and was swinging it like a sword. When it drew nearer, Nick tossed several glass shards from the broken window at it. As the creature raised its arm to block the attack, Nick took the brief distraction as an opportunity to grab hold of its arm and snap the elbow joint. Unfortunately, the beast still refused to release the staff, and instead raised Nick toward its other hand so it could rain a few more punches down on the out-muscled hero.

Nearby, Hood was heavily outnumbered, and as much as she loved a challenge, this one was getting out of hand. She was stabbing and slicing as fast as she could but her arms were getting tired and the creatures were getting closer. She looked over to Nick, hoping he was nearly done.

Nick reached for the lever on his staff through the flurry of punches and pressed it, which shot a knife down through the giant's foot and jammed into the floor. He then grabbed a shard of glass still sticking out of its chest and began swiping at its wrists and ankles. At last, his staff clattered to the floor as the giant's grip began to fail, and its legs were soon to follow as it collapsed onto its knees. Nick snatched the staff, leapt up onto the giant's shoulders as it reached up to grab him again. He raised his weapon—with the knife end pointing toward his victim—and coldly plunged the blade into its forehead. The massive being quivered for a moment, then was still.

As Nick breathed a sigh of relief, he caught sight of Hood, who was being pushed back inside the house. He watched as she threw another dagger into the eyeball of a zombie, and saw the look of panic cross her face as she realized it was her last. Before Nick could get to her, she was set upon by two of the hoard, one biting her neck, another on her leg. Nick watched a third zombie sprint inside the house before Blitzen swooped down holding the rest of the army at bay with her powerful flames. Nick waited until he saw the zombie run past the window then javelined his staff to bore a hole through the creature as well as the other two that had grabbed hold of Hood. He leaped inside to reclaim his weapon, which had pinned the three zombies to the wall, before inspecting Hood. Despite the bites and blood pouring out of her, she seemed all right, just a little tired. Hood tried to stand but stumbled for a moment before collapsing back to the floor.

Nick sat down next to her and cradled her head. "Why did you have to come here?" he shook his head, trying to smile as the tears welled in his eyes. "You work alone, remember?"

"What can I say, you're growing on me, Nicky," she said. "But you're lucky I'm so sleepy coz you know I hate being touched."

Nick chuckled and glanced up to see Blitzen still holding back the crowd. "Yeah, well, you can get me back later Red Riding Hood," he smiled and looked down at her, but her last breath was leaving her lips as he spoke.

His emotions swirled between anger and despair. Anger at the zombies for taking her, and himself for not being faster. Despair that they'd spent 100 years apart, but couldn't have more than five minutes together. It wasn't fair.

Suddenly Hood cut through his breakdown as she rose sharply to attack him, now as a zombie with the singular goal of replenishing her lost blood supply through mass food consumption. Nick jumped back and tried to keep his distance. They were an even match physically, but she was certainly quicker now that the zombie bug was doing its thing. Hood lunged at Nick, who ducked and blocked as much as he could, not wanting to land any punches himself as he battled for a solution. Meanwhile Hood was not holding back, throwing kick after punch after kick in quick succession. Nick took a few shots to the chest and a solid kick to the hip which knocked him sideways.

He ducked under another kick, deflected a punch and wrapped her in a curtain to buy himself some time. One thing in his favor was her aggression—slightly higher than usual—was making her careless, and he had his chances to retaliate if he wanted.

Nick racked his brain, thinking back to all the stories his dad had told, and to his mother's training, and then had an idea. *The kiss!* When his mother had first turned, Claws kissed her, which stopped the disease in its tracks, and the same with Mortus when they faced off in their fight. *I have that dragon breath in me, too*, he plotted. *So maybe...*

Nick knew his breath wasn't as strong as Claws'. Perhaps it was the Viking blood in the old man's veins that offered the perfect fuel for the dragon fire. Who knew. But Nick didn't need it to be as strong as his dad's. It just had to be strong enough to save Hood.

He waited for the young woman to untangle from the blinds and charge at him. This time instead of blocking or dodging, Nick opened his arms and embraced Hood, pressing his lips firmly to hers. He wasn't game to use tongue in case the idea didn't work, but he blew as much air down her throat as her lungs would take. He hugged her for a moment as she growled and squirmed until at last she relaxed. Nick eased back from his hug and found his girl staring back at him, albeit dazed and pale, but human.

Hood tried to say something but passed out—not surprising given the ordeal and the growing puddle of blood beneath her. Nick threw her over his shoulder and walked up to Blitzen who was really starting to struggle with keeping her flames going. He tossed the girl onto the dragon's back and patted Blitzen on his head. "Get her out of here for me, girl," he shouted over the sound of the raging battle.

The dragon took off, leaving Nick to resume hostilities. With Hood now safe, he looked back inside the house to see flames leaking through from the front where his father had been fighting. "Dad, are you OK?" he bellowed into the corridor.

22

CRISP KRINGLE

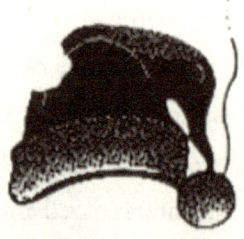

The wooden doors of the burning sheep cupboard soon began to blacken as the smoldering prisoners lit up their cell. Claws stepped back as the flames leaked through the cracks and could feel a deep rumble shaking through the ground. Realizing this was not the work of his captive fireballs, he ran back to the door and thrust it open. From the rear of the swarming sea of monsters, Claws saw a stampede of cattle charging the house. Zombie or not they would be trouble enough as they were, but then the dragons—while burning some nearby attackers—caught a few cows with their flames. At least now he knew where to send the thank-you cards for the burning lamb chops that attacked him earlier. His own team were lighting them up!

To his horror, Claws watched as one burning cow bumped another, which in turn lit up and bumped another, and so on until a whole herd of burning plus-sized barbecue steaks found themselves hurtling in his direction. Claws turned quickly and yelled back down the hall.

"Nick, you might want to start heading back, son!" But as Claws yelled, he noticed the strangest thing happen and—though recent events had certainly altered what he once considered strange—even *he* had to admit that this was a departure from his widening acceptance of normality. For when he spoke, the flames of the burning door leaped across and briefly ignited his breath. Claws considered the phenomenon for a moment and then turned towards the swarm of zombies. He stepped back behind the flames and sucked in a lungful of that burning gas he had endured for so long. He tensed his chest, opened his lips and blew out as hard as he could, sending streams of flames swirling out over the balcony and burning any zombie within range. Another gift from his reptilian wingmen.

It was an amazing effect that halted the zombie army. Ruled by instinct in their primitive form, it seemed their brains were wired to avoid unnecessary forays into raging infernos, and Claws was happy to offer them every chance to overcome it.

Suddenly Nick came dashing in from the kitchen, excited and out of breath, and stood in the hallway next to the sheep cupboard. "Hey, Pops, are you still alive...?" he began, but his voice trailed off as he caught a glimpse of his father's light show.

Suddenly he was wrenched from his trance by the sheep bursting through the brittle doors right in front of him. Significantly burned but still moving—albeit dragging their paralyzed hind legs and struggling to breath—the zombie sheep set their sights on the hunter-in-training and made a desperate lunge in his direction. Before Nick had a chance to even react, Claws jumped in and killed the two sheep with a devastating strike from his flails.

"Kid, you have so much to learn. Now, come on, we need to get upstairs."

Nick looked at the advancing zombies and smirked. "Why? We can take these guys." His confidence was clearly on the rise as he readied his staff for the fight. That was until the quickest of the blazing herd of cattle came bursting through the front of the house and smashed down the hallway, narrowly missing them both. Claws grabbed the dumbfounded Nick and dragged him toward the stairs. The cattle continued to smash through the house as the two men dodged their way to the bottom step.

Within inches of their target, a large bull smashed through the front wall and made a beeline for the boys. With nowhere to go, Claws grabbed Nick by the collar and hurled him up the first ten steps onto a landing as the bull barreled into his own chest and pushed him all the way down the corridor. Another bull then rushed through and smashed the bottom of the stairs, with Claws narrowly avoiding its hooves as he picked himself up off the ground.

He got to his feet in a fair bit of pain and stumbled to the staircase, but it was like swimming against a raging river of acid. For every two steps he took forward, he got knocked back another five by the stampede running through the living room, not to mention the pain of his burning flesh was excruciating. Then he had an idea. As the next bull charged toward him, he jumped to one side, and latched onto its horns with his flail before turning the creature sharply into the nearby wall. It slammed to a halt and narrowly missed crushing Claws' arm. The desired effect was soon to follow as the surging cattle began to trip over the new obstacle and pile up in the hallway.

As the beasts began to fall, Claws jumped up onto their backs and navigated his way across them towards the staircase like he was crossing hot coals to prove his manhood. Only these 'coals' were hot fatty harbingers of bovine necrosis, and he wasn't so much as proving his manhood as trying to save it from being trampled or burnt. The elevation of his new steppingstones was just high enough for Nick to reach down and help swing his father up onto the landing, and as the two struggled their way to the top, the cattle below soon began moo-ving again.

Flames and livestock continued to ravage the lower levels of the home, and the two men could feel the foundations growing increasingly unstable. The zombie army had begun trying to scale the outer walls of the house, while inside they were working on the staircase. So far, the odd one that succeeded was quickly dispatched and thrown back to the ground but for each body that fell, it simply brought the next zombie closer as they climbed their fallen comrades to get nearer their foe.

Nick put out his arm to show his dad a bitemark slowly healing up. "On the plus side," he smiled despite his exhaustion. "It looks like all those years wrestling with Ralph finally paid off. They can't turn me."

Soon the pile of zombie bodies was high enough for every approaching assailant to climb up to attack them. They raced up the stairs and poured in through the windows. The boys fought bravely against the surrounding swarm. Back to back, fighting with flails and staff and flaming breath, they operated with seamless efficiency, as if some unspoken connection of their minds allowed them to know exactly where the other was moving and where the next attack was required.

Their movements were like a well-rehearsed dance, but as good as they were, the circle continued to tighten, and the creatures were drawing in. They both knew where the battle was heading but there was little option other than to push on or be slaughtered sooner.

So, Claws and Nick fought on.

The zombies continued streaming through every opening, with more and more cramming into the room each second. A beam nearby fell from the roof and crushed a few attackers. A section of floor crashed away near a window from the furnace roaring below, taking out a few more monsters. But the losses were like drops in the ocean, and the valiant pair were drowning fast.

Eventually, the heroes neared their end. The zombie hoard was almost upon them, their energy was spent, and the bruises were adding up faster than their healing powers could rectify. Claws took a heavy shot to the face and fell to the floor. Nick swung across in front of him with his staff to hold off the crowd on his father's side but that left his own back exposed and he was viciously slashed by a broken bottle. As Nick fell to the ground, his father sought vengeance as best he could by smashing the legs of his aggressors as he lay on the floor.

Nick took a bite to the ankle. Claws struggled to remove one from his arm. Their blood still sizzled and burned the zombies on contact, but it barely slowed them down. This army was on a mission, and in moments it would be complete. In the distance they could hear Ralph cry out in pain, but not even that could inspire enough energy for them to break free and save the beast.

Soon the pair were covered in bites as the zombies piled on to rip them apart. The sky above them darkened with undead bodies blocking out the sun. As Claws closed his eyes, he felt a sense of weightlessness overcome him, this must have been what death felt like. It had come for him finally. He floated for a moment in silent acceptance. Heaven, hell, or somewhere in between was calling for him and he was ready. Then he began to drop. *Not surprising,* he thought, *given I've basically fought and killed for a living most of my life.* But he really thought his recent good Samaritan streak might have earned him a ticket upstairs.

As he felt the flames of hell getting nearer, suddenly someone grabbed hold of his arm and he stopped. He opened his eyes to find himself hanging through a huge hole in the floor and Nick straining to hold on. "You're not dead yet old man," he grunted and hoisted Claws back up.

Several zombies had plummeted through the floor when the section below them gave way around one beam on which the pair now sat. This had opened a narrow path to the window, and the men took their chance. With Claws' weapons lost somewhere to the depths of the house, the two men held Nick's staff together to make their final push, scattering any zombie between them and freedom as they edged their way along the beam. With zombies falling left and right into the first floor fire, Claws and Nick limped toward the window. Behind them more of the floor gave way, and not seconds after their feet left the beam to jump outside, did their wooden saviour also disappear. The whole house began to groan as its very foundations strained under the weight of the inferno.

They jumped out on to the roof of the lower level and fought off more zombies as they looked down at the army below with the sun now peeping over the horizon. "See, everything has an end," Claws said, trying to reassure his tiring sidekick as they saw the vast crowd before them had been reduced to half its size. Finally, they had made a dent in the attack. Of course, that still left them with a considerable force to reckon with, but it was still a small boost to their confidence.

Just then the house began to shake. The pillars snapped on the balcony below them, and the far wall of the house collapsed in on itself. They felt their side begin to lean and fall toward the army. As the house tipped over, their rooftop dropped closer and closer to the ground until it hit, and the two men tumbled off it onto the ground.

Eventually they rolled to a stop and wearily climbed to their feet. As they looked around them, the army of zombies surrounded them like rabid bloodhounds waiting for their master to command the attack, each one still clinging to a hint of their former lives. Doctors swung stethoscopes like nunchucks, farmers carried pitchforks and shovels, artists wielded... paint brushes? In the distance they could see the dragons, being netted one-by-one by the zombies, and dragged down from the air. The town burned with flaming livestock still rampaging through the streets, lending a hellish glow to the brightening skies above. Perhaps they had fallen further than they thought. But the devil who owned this particular playground was a figure all too familiar to them.

"Ha, ha, ha," came the confident cackling of their primary target. The two men quickly scanned for their weapons, but they were nowhere to be seen. "If you're looking for your toys, I wouldn't bother," Mortus assured them. "They've been scattered across this courtyard as your lifeless husks will soon be as well."

The villain clapped twice, and his army dragged Ralph over to their King. The dragon was covered in blood from multiple cuts and his breathing was shallow. Mortus grabbed the creature and held a knife to its throat and laughed as Claws rushed forward with Nick close behind. Suddenly the zombie army snapped into action, stepping to block the path of the heroes and holding them back. Claws looked confused as to what Mortus found so funny.

"You idiots, do you really think I couldn't work out your little secret?" Mortus bragged cockily. "How to get the gas without copping the heat? You try going face to face with a normal dragon and you might as well be playing Russian roulette with a clip full of bullets. They have to want to hurt you to even let this stuff out of their body. But your little pet's defect reduces those odds by half."

Ralph suddenly fired a burst of flame into a nearby minion. Mortus simply smirked. "Of course, I want a little more assurance than that so draining the blood helps to tire them out a little and they can't throw out a spark. Those effects are amplified with this guy," he tousled Ralph's mane, "who never had a great deal of control to begin with," Mortus began to lean his face toward the dragon but Ralph let out a much smaller flame, causing the evil one to hesitate angrily.

"No!" he scolded and stabbed the dragon in the neck. The dragon wailed and slumped to the ground. "Safety first," Mortus sneered.

He then gripped Ralph's face and inhaled his breath as the dragon growled and tried weakly to fight back, but no fire came out. Mortus' body surged with energy at the rejuvenating effect of the pure unignited gas. His leg painfully yet satisfyingly healed at long last and he tossed his cane far away into the crowd.

"Your breath was a good short-term hit, Claws, but the real deal really puts a more permanent pep in your step," he buzzed. Another few zombies followed suit before Ralph was able to fire and incinerated one of the creatures.

Mortus was unfazed and turned to Claws who was smiling at Ralph's little revenge. "No matter," he said calmly. "I have plenty more." Mortus jammed the knife into Ralph's neck and the creature roared. "I told you that was naughty," he scolded. "Don't do that again."

Suddenly coal pellets splattered into the Zombie King like a paintball gun on overdrive, as Larry, Pete and Shirly dropped down into the field. The King stumbled backward as the coal spread across his body, while the elves set to work picking off as many zombie bystanders as they could hit. They were shredding the army as they flipped around the troops. A few pellets even struck the zombies around Claws and he started to work his way free.

But as quickly as hope was delivered, it again was snatched away when a golf club smashed Larry into a waiting box held by a newly enhanced zombie minion. "Four!" came the mocking call of the Zombie King as the last bits of coal crumbled away from his shoulder. Pete and Shirly followed soon after as the super powered zombies completed their collection and dunked it under water. Now if the elves tried to break free they would drown in the process.

Nick and Claws again tried to rescue their friends despite several zombies already pinning them down. But the King was now stepping things up. The men could only watch as the zombies continued to pull the trigger on their life or death game with Ralph's unpredictable flame. Some burned in a heap while others were supercharged by the gas.

They watched helplessly as Ralph grew weaker and they were punched, kicked and scratched on the ground. The dragon wailed in pain. He couldn't take much more, and neither could they. Nick collapsed after a few successive hits to the jaw, and slowly slipped from consciousness, while Claws threw himself over his son to shield his body. The zombies rained down their attacks. More of the dragons were caught. It seemed the battle was over and there were no falling floors or beams to save them this time.

Just when all hope appeared lost, something dropped from the sky and crashed to the ground next to them in a huge cloud of ash. That cloud exploded in every direction, surrounding the boys and turning every nearby zombie it touched into dust as it cleared a path to their so-called King.

Above them, Blitzen spread her wings and rose back up into the air.

By the time the ash cloud reached Mortus, it had faded away to a wispy wave washing over his feet. His skin sizzled softly as the few specks brushed his ankles. As the cloud dissipated, seven powerful-looking zombies stood by the dragon. Pieces of coal and ash crumbled from their bodies. A few hundred more of the regular zombies were scattered about the field, sheltered by random pieces of equipment and fallen debris or simply too far out of range of the deadly cloud.

Claws and his son slowly sat up rubbing their heads. Those hits must have been harder than they thought because even with their healing powers in overdrive, they could swear they were seeing something impossible.

Rising from the center of the cloud now stood Befana. And she looked pissed.

23

SLAY MY NAME

Befana rose to her feet from the middle of the cloud and looked back at her family, a monstrous look had engulfed her face, and pure rage pulsed through her system. "Stay out of my way," she snarled aggressively. Claws and Nick shared a look of concern as she turned to walk away—lost again, it seemed, to the disease after all those years of progress. Then, however, she stopped and thought for a second, before adding with a smile, "My darlings." It may have been intended as a sweet little gesture, but it looked creepy as hell in reality. Still, maybe she wasn't so far gone.

Mortus turned to Befana with a smile. "My, my, Mrs Claws, it's good to see you out of that frosty cage. How long has it be-" Befana cut him short by whipping out her bow and shooting a charcoal arrow, causing him to dive out of the way. The missile whizzed past Mortus towards a zombie that had been crawling out from behind a rock. No sooner had it risen to its feet, did the arrow imbed itself into the creature's chest. This time, the coal did not spread externally across the creature's skin, but instead spewed through every orifice as its organs turned to dust. By the time it crashed back down behind the rock it was nothing more than a puff of black dust wafting up into the air, and a pile of ash spilling out into the open.

Mortus coolly dusted himself off and continued his rant as Befana eased back the string of her bow, conjuring another dirt black arrow ready to fire, as again she took aim at the King. "Anyway, as I was saying, I've..." he began, before Befana launched another arrow at him. This time, he dragged a nearby minion to block its path. The arrow plunged into the minion's chest and the wound spread both inside and out. The creature's eyes filled with darkness, until they popped in its skull, then it too collapsed in a smoldering, sizzling pile of ash on the ground.

Mortus continued his disjointed proclamation as he leaped behind a few zombies scattered around battlefield to shield himself from Befana, who rattled off several more quick shots in succession.

"I've come... a long way... since you left... me for dead," he stuttered.

As the last rotting corpse vaporized in his hands, the zombie leader paused to regroup. His mood turned to anger as the ashen cloud of zombie bits dissipated, and he and Befana stared each other down.

"Would you let me finish?!" he barked as blood rushed to his eyes and that demonic sneer crept up his face.

"You're next," she growled as she marched through the dusty field toward him, firing one more arrow as she advanced. This time, one of the enhanced minions stepped into the firing line. The arrow hit the creature in the chest and sliced through the skin, but as the coal crackled and fell away, the creature was healing underneath.

Mortus smiled as the fruits of his labors came to bear. "Perfect," he crowed, "my army is complete." Now seemingly just as keen to resume hostilities, and safe in the knowledge these arrows presented no terminal threat to him, Mortus sprang towards Befana to engage. His scattered minions reacted as if waking from a stunned trance and launched at Claws and Nick, while the enhanced few formed up around their king.

Claws scanned for a weapon among the implements and spotted an old friend nearby. "Grab a shovel!" he called to Nick as he picked up a particularly battered looking implement and spun it with a smile. As a zombie closed in, he swung hard at the creature, but unfortunately the old wood just shattered on its head, and he was left holding the handle like a jagged wooden knuckle duster.

As disappointing as it was, it did grant him a few seconds to think, and he spotted the zombie holding his elven friends hostage. Claws kicked up a pitchfork from the ground and launched it into the chest of the creature, which flew backward, ripping its hand and the box it was holding, out of the water. No sooner was their prison dry did the dark elves explode from the wood, and wasted no time in jamming every piece of shattered material they could find into the zombie's body like a lethal dose of acupuncture. No amount of healing power was going to save that thing as it convulsed for a moment on the floor, before Shirly smashed a toy boat through its nasal cavity to disengage the brain.

"Larry, get to Befana," came the call from Mr Claws as he was set upon again by more zombies. It didn't take any further convincing for the elves to ditch the great red slayer and help his wife with the King. Perhaps they had grown to respect Claws' authority on the battlefield and follow his instruction. Or they just liked Befana more.

"Hey dad," Nick chuckled nearby as his spade swung perfectly at a few approaching targets. "You're right about these things. They work great!" Claws stabbed and slashed with his shattered short-range spike as he watched Nick maneuver his tool as expertly as *he* had done so many years before. It may have been the near-certain concussion talking, but a feeling of pride bubbled up through the blood filling the old man's lungs as he watched his boy go to work and, though it hurt too much to smile, deep down he grinned from ear to ear.

As the dark elves joined Befana, they began pushing back the zombie hoard and establishing a little arena where the warrior could go to work. The few 'regular' zombies that chose to fight Befana were easily dispatched with some quick-fire ashen arrows, before she split her razor-sharp bow and sliced the remaining undead with gracefully terrifying ease.

She then met King Mortus, now surrounded by a pack of superpowered bodyguards. Befana struck and sliced each of the foe, causing them to briefly retreat with massive damage, but their healing powers kept them coming back virtually unscathed. They still couldn't feel any pain—this had taken Befana years of exposure just to begin to maintain any long-term sensations—but the dragon gas now inside this crew was certainly capable of at least healing these superficial injuries, and fast.

Soon Mortus drew a second sword and joined the fray as the pair began a rapid battle of blades amid the crowd. It seemed this deathless affliction, while dulling many of their other senses, had also forged a path to greater focus on the primitive tasks, such as combat, that remained. Like clearing a forest in their minds to just a few tall trees, they saw clearly what they were doing with nothing slowing them down.

Their hands were a blur with the sparks and pings of striking metal. The two battled throughout the arena like the immortal beings they were, taking hits without pain and causing widespread damage at breakneck speed. While Befana had the advantage in speed and was by far the better fighter, she had to also contend with the odd interruption of the King's zombie minions, and needed the added milliseconds to react and dispatch them before he struck again. Not without a deadly catch of his own, Mortus could seemingly dig deeper into those adrenal reserves, allowing himself to give in to his darker desires that Befana still tried to resist. This gave him a decided power advantage, and he carelessly destroyed nearby houses and carts they passed with a single swing of his arm. He even gladly sacrificed his own kind, tossing them at his opponent to slow her down.

As quick as Befana was, these empowered minions didn't go down as easily as the others. Her arrows just crumbled from their bodies. Their injuries healed. What bought her the most time was taking chunks out of their legs as these took a few minutes to grow back.

Every so often, when she managed to thin the crowd a little, Befana took a moment to jam her bow back together and clear a few zombies from around her struggling husband and son who were being overrun by the undead.

But as quick as she was, even she could not keep this up. She needed to even the odds.

Befana parried a few more shots from the self-pro-claimed King before kicking a nearby enhanced in the chest, sending it crashing through the brick wall of a barn. She then shot an arrow through the fresh new hole and shattered the main supporting beam, causing the entire structure to fall in and crush the creature.

With not a second to spare she was then rocked by a powerful kick from another minion, then struck in the face by two more as she crashed to the ground and her bow slid away. Enraged by the cheap shot, she booted the kneecap of the nearest enhanced, which gave a sickening crack as jagged bone poked through the skin. She then grabbed the shattered leg and forced the creature to knee another in the throat with its broken bone, and they fell to the ground with one still embedded in the other.

As they squirmed on the floor, she kicked the embedded knee once more, causing the bone to rip through the neck of the fallen zombie before retrieving her razor-sharp bow and slicing off the head of the other one.

Even the King stopped to witness the gruesome dispatch and he couldn't help but feel a little concerned. Befana could see it in his eyes and grinned wickedly as she brushed back her hair. She took a moment to check in on her strug-gling family.

"I see your father taught you how to fight," she called to Nick as he was punched in the face by a zombie. He angrily kneed the creature in the jaw and threw it back into the crowd. He used the shovel to break off the tip of a rake lying nearby before stepping on the head causing it to flip up just as a zombie lunged toward him, impaling itself on the rising freshly serrated end. He then shattered his shovel on another zombie and was tackled to the ground by two more.

"He may have shown me a few things," he panted as he wrestled with them.

Befana ran at the shaken Mortus and kicked him in the chest. She then leaned back to stab an enhanced zombie behind her in the chest with the end of her bow before swinging back to protect herself from the King's next attack. Her focus was now so intense that she was moving as if time itself almost stood still. In one fluid motion she blocked the King's next shot before spinning around to sweep the legs out from under the zombie she just stabbed behind her. Before it had a chance to fall, she rolled underneath the airborne undead—as if crawling under a table—and gutted another nearby enhanced with a slash of its stomach as it joined the fight, simultaneously dodging the King as he leaped forward with a forceful stab of his sword.

Unfortunately for him, Mortus embedded his blade in the guts of the 'table zombie' and could only watch in amazement as Befana emerged from her cover. At lightning speed, she stepped on the shoulder of the freshly gutted enhanced—which had now doubled over, not from pain but lack of stomach muscles—then jumped up onto the falling table zombie, which currently housed the King's sword in its breastplate as he tried to pull it free. Befana kicked the sword from his hand and used it to remove the heads of both her table and the gutless enhanced still trying to gather its entrails from the floor. With the minions dispatched, she waited atop the falling body like an elevator descending to the ground, with her newly acquired blade pointed at the Zombie King. And in just those few seconds, the battle was over.

When the table-turned-elevator hit the ground, she smiled mockingly through some heavy breaths, calling back to her son. "Advanced training's this way, if you're interested, boys," she called. Mortus opened his mouth to speak, but she quickly shut that down, slashing the King across the chest before kicking him backward and throwing the sword, which dug its blade half an inch into his skull.

After a moment, Mortus closed his eyes and chuckled to himself as blood trickled down from the wound. "I don't think they heard you."

Befana glanced in the direction of the boys as the pair disappeared amid a pile of zombies. She quickly turned and fired a bunch of arrows at the offenders while running towards them, burning a hole through the crowd that let her see the two boys for a moment before more zombies joined the pile and buried them again.

As she ran, the last two enhanced zombies tried to block her path, each one brandishing sharp twisted farming implements they must have ripped from a plough. As they swung their weapons, she effortlessly slid toward them on her knees to dodge the strikes, slicing each of their legs with her bow before standing up between them and removing their heads as they began to fall. She noticed Nick's staff on the ground and snatched it up, javelining it into the back of a zombie climbing the pile.

Suddenly, something pulled the staff through from inside and the two men burst out, both brandishing the weapon and pushing back the zombies together. To their right Befana saw another minion sneaking up on Claws, but this one was dragging his flail along the ground. Befana, close now, launched herself at the group, shooting a line of arrows through the air and striking the rising arm of the zombie before it could swing the weapon down on Claws' head. She crashed into the charcoal statue, dropping the flail into the waiting arm of her husband, as she rolled to a stop next to her boys. The three stood together with weapons in hand facing the remaining zombies surrounding them. Considering what they had already faced, the remaining stragglers posed little threat and were easily dispatched as the family closed out the battle together.

With the coast now clear, Befana looked out over the battlefield to find the King, but he was nowhere to be seen.

The family shared a brief hug in relief and exhaustion, though they couldn't shake the frustration that their target had escaped again.

"How did you know to come find us?" asked Nick, as he turned to his mother.

"I told you," she smiled. "If you ran into trouble, I'd know about it." She looked behind Nick, prompting the young hero to turn his gaze, and there stood Hood. Not looking 100 percent her best—and there were a few elves nearby keeping watch in case anything changed—but she was still sporting that confident smile he just couldn't get enough of.

"She may have had some help," Hood grinned weakly.

"Why this time?" Claws asked curiously. He had put himself in many stupid predicaments before, and none convinced Befana to take this chance and leave the nest. So what had changed?

"I met a young girl who said that being alone sucks, and all she wanted now was a family. It made me realize, it *does*. So why should I sit at home alone worrying about you, when I could be out here doing something about it. It's not like you don't need saving... all the time." she smiled, holding up three fingers, then four, five, six and laughed. Claws saw a genuine look of peace in her eyes that had been missing for decades.

Before his musings could stretch to a second sentence, a bleeding mess suddenly dropped from the sky, and Ralph landed semi-gracefully next to it with the dark elves on his back. The dragon picked up the groaning, squirming body in his mouth and dragged it toward them before giving it a hard shake like a dog trying to silence its favorite chew toy. Claws walked up with a smile and patted the proud creature on the head as it dropped the prize at his feet. Claws rolled the body onto its back to see the familiar scarred face of Mortus smiling despite some massive injuries.

"Well, well, I do believe we have some catching up to do, Morty," said Claws, who raised an evil grin.

Mortus looked unfazed. "Oh, Claws, just give up. You can't win."

Claws stepped on Morty's leg as he crouched down to try and inflict some pain. "Well, I'd be lying if I said I wasn't enjoying the challenge," he sneered.

The King looked down at his now broken leg as it silently healed. "You can't break what's already broken Claws. You can beat me up all you want but nothing is going to make up for what I did to her, or you to me," he laughed. "I feel nothing! You wanna kill me? Who cares? I will die a peaceful death and your heart, which aches for revenge, will feel as numb as I have since *you* did this to me," he raged with near psychotic fury.

Claws took a breath and crouched before his adversary, just as they had done on the cliffs a century ago. "Oh you wanna *feel* something Morty?" Claws warned as he suddenly breathed out, giving Mortus a deep breath of his rejuvenating air. "All you had to do was ask."

The Zombie King squirmed in agony as the feeling returned to his beaten extremities—every broken bone and shredded skin cell screaming through his tattered nervous system. Mortus writhed on the ground, feeling his mangled body rip apart to be sewn back together. "You took everything from me." Mortus cried angrily through the pain. "I was respected, admired, and I was loyal to you," he panted. Claws' face slowly dropped as he listened. "Yet still, you, my friend, after 10 years stripped it all away for some piece of ass you knew for 10 minutes, leaving me with nothing." The pain had subsided now as Mortus sat up and stared at Claws, still trying to catch his breath. Claws' mind was racing, searching his memory, reliving his past. "You want to know who the real villain is here?" Morty coldly concluded. "Then take a look at yourself."

Nick lost his temper and took a step towards Mortus but Claws, clearly struggling to contain some new emotion of his own, put an arm out to hold him back.

"Wait Nick, he's..." Claws stumbled over his words, taken aback as the realization of his actions began to take a toll. He thought back over those many years hunting, and could barely remember spending another moment with the man now sitting at his feet. Was Morty right? Had his pride and ego been responsible for his friend's demise? Was he to blame for this corrupted asshole now lying before him?

"Look Morty, I'm sorry," said Claws, flattened, confused and consumed by a flood of guilt as Frankenstein now stared at his monster. He'd tried so hard these last 100 years to redeem himself from his dragon slaying days, yet after all this time he still found himself back at the Pole with the dragon mother dying in his arms. He knew if he couldn't let this obsession for revenge get out of his head, he would never find his way out of that cave. With a glance toward Befana he knew even she, the greatest wronged by the man laying before them, agreed.

Claws sighed as he wandered over to Mortus. "You know you were right before." Claws said sadly as he extended a hand to help Morty to his feet. "You can't break what's already broken, and we *are* broken my friend. I may never be able to forgive my own part in what you've become, and I don't expect you to either. But an old friend once told me that failure is just the first step in every new adventure. So, let's see where this takes us. Let us help you."

Mortus was surprised, but not ready to back down. "You can't just fix me Claws."

"Maybe we can," Claws theorised. "Befana was able to beat this disease. It's not too late for you."

"I'm still going to kill you." Morty promised.

"Morty come on," Claws begged. "You're not a fighter, you hate that stuff."

"The only thing I hate is-"

"Me, yeah I got it," Claws finished his sentence. "Look, there's no more hiding behind desensitized fists anymore. If you want to keep fighting me, you will feel every blow. I'm giving you a chance to choose your own path here." Claws turned away from him and walked back to his family. "Just think about it at least."

"Oh shut up with the high and mighty routine, you oaf! You couldn't just stay a stupid puppet, could you?" Mortus spat the words as if they tasted as foul as they sounded. "Just play the part, swing your fists and do as you're told? You had to go and grow a pair and try to be a real boy. Well, you failed. You watch your back, Santa," he mocked, trying to get a reaction. "Because the next time that wife of yours goes gift-giving or your boy picks up a whore, they just might not come back. I'll make sure of it." Claws remained quiet. Mortus taunted him further, trying to re-engage him. "I'll make a new army. This will never be over!"

Mortus pulled a knife from his belt and tried to launch himself at Claws, but his hand was instantly struck with a charcoal pellet from Larry, before Nick's staff whizzed by and severed the limb as Befana stepped between them and pushed him back with one hand. Then Ralph bit down on Mortus' shoulder and sat him back on the ground.

Claws turned back toward Morty. "Well, this is *my* army," he threatened. "And yes, it is over. You may have heard a rumor going around that I don't have a lot of time for people that don't want to play nice. And it seems pretty clear you're set on staying on that list."

Claws nodded to Ralph and the bloodied dragon bit into the arm of the King, its big eye staring straight into his. "Ow!" Mortus winced. He was not enjoying this reunion with pain.

Ralph then lifted him up and away to where the other dragons were waiting to tear him apart. "So, if you'll excuse us," Claws called out to him. "My little dragons need to borrow you for a while."

Claws smiled, kissed his wife, and put his arm around his family as they began walking down the empty street off into the horizon—the screams of the Zombie King echoing through the town. As they passed a timid Hood, Claws extended his arms for her to join their group hug and she gladly tucked under his wing next to Nick.

"Dad, were you worried we were going to die back there?" Nick innocently quizzed.

"The thought never crossed my mind, son," came the cool reply.

They walked a moment longer.

"Is that coz you knew Mom would save us?" Nick continued.

"Your mother put you up to this didn't she?" said Claws, maintaining his bravado.

They continued to walk.

"She's really good, isn't she, Dad?" Nick smiled.

Claws pulled up and began walking back toward the battlefield. "You know what? I'm going to go see if the dragons are still hungry." He called out to the dragons. "Hey guys, save room for dessert!"

Befana laughed and called out to him. "So that's about 20 you owe me now, by the way."

Ignoring her, Claws sarcastically called to the dragons "On second thought, if you're hungry I hear there's this mean old lady and some wise-ass kids down the street that could be worth a snack."

Befana smiled and put her arm around her family, as they continued walking together. Perhaps it was the dragon breath surging through her system, or the years of her body's gradual rejuvenation, or her newfound pride in herself and her family, or maybe even just the afternoon spent letting off steam and killing zombies—but she was definitely feeling better than she had in a very long time.

24

HAPPILY NEVER AFTER

AKA THE SEQUEL

The burning bodies of cattle lay strewn around the broken homestead where Claws had made his stand. As the last twitching bull lay still and slipped finally into an eternal state of slumber, the hero caught up with, and rejoined his family on the slow march from town, leaving it all to just rot in his wake.

With a sharp whistle he called his dragons to follow, and they dutifully tossed aside the remains of their foe to take flight in pursuit of their master. The elves—now finished transforming the legion of charcoaled undead—hitched a ride as they passed and as the whoosh of their wings faded into the distance, the town fell silent once more.

A few sparks crackled in the softly burning timbers of the house, and every so often another piece would fall from the roof and tumble into the flames. Eventually, one lone bull suddenly climbed to its feet and shook its body to extinguish the flames, like a dog emerging from a fishpond.

It watched the vanishing silhouette of the attackers dissolving into the sunset, and sighed before quietly transforming into a deep black scaly dragon and wandering over to the mutilated remains of the Zombie King.

The dragons had not left much behind. A portion of his face and skull clung to the top of the spinal column. His one dead eye—twisted in an agonized screech—stared blankly into the distance, too far gone for his inherited healing powers to repair. The dragon took a moment to inspect the body before leaning down and breathing onto the remains. It sizzled and hissed as it began to regenerate. Cell by cell it worked its way along the severed edges of the skull like pulling the thread of a cardigan played in reverse.

Tissue began wrapping itself around the spine as the dragon continued to blow on the corpse, before the torso grew and fattened around it. Limbs then sprouted like seedlings pushing through the dirt.

The eye then suddenly twitched to life again and began searching around, soaked in the freshly exhaled regenerative breath, and as the voice box took shape, a groan became a growl then a shout of pain. Soon the Zombie King was reformed, and he rose to his feet, still twisting and turning his limbs to realign his freshly constructed form.

"Dragon!" he shouted once his mind had adjusted to its reanimation, and he set to defend himself. When it didn't attack, he looked at the creature for a moment, and could see that there was something different about this one. "You're not one of them," he stared quizzically at his redeemer. "Who are you?"

The dragon took its cue to begin its own transformation. It rose up on its hind legs as thick hair spurted out across its body, charcoal black with a tinge of navy blue. Its muscles bulged in its legs with feet expanding to rip through its scaly claws. Two razor-sharp teeth wriggled out through its lips while a pair of shoulder-length ears slid their way down its back.

"So, the stories are true," said the King in awe of the giant beast. He extended a hand to shake its paw. "Mr Bunny, I presume?"

The prehistoric rabbit did not return his gesture. It had walked this earth for thousands of years, surviving world-ending meteors and extinction-level freezes, and most recently, a little late afternoon barbeque, so such gestures of goodwill were far too flippant to indulge as their long-term resonance would be minimal.

It simply tossed the claw necklace to the Zombie King and stared at him intently. The King gripped the necklace and remembered his pain, as they basked for a moment in the shared hatred of their common enemy.

"I hear you loud and clear," he growled.

Then with one giant punch of its feet, the rabbit leaped into the air and disappeared over the horizon.

Don't Go Yet!

Ok, so yes, the book is now finished and our time has inevitably come to an end.

Whether it was a genuine interest in my writing, laziness to choose something else to read, or the Stockholm syndrome finally kicking in, I am very thankful you have made it this far.

So before you go:

Would you please leave this book an honest review on whichever retailer was crazy enough to stock it? Maybe even tell a friend, neighbour, or jump on the latest social media platform to post, tweet, blog, DM, hashtag, grind, snap or swipe this thing into the hearts and minds of anyone who will listen.

Reviews are an essential part of the author ecosystem and helps other readers fall into my trap – I mean, find my book – which in turn lets me keep writing more and spreading my madness like a plague until the whole world is at last under my spell.

It only takes a minute to go tell a friend or leave a review.

All joking and dreams of world domination aside, I genuinely appreciate your time and support. This has been a 10 year battle that my whole family has jumped on board to help me finish this book. So I can't thank *them* enough for getting me here, and *you* for taking a chance on reading the scribbled ramblings of a new author to the game.

I look forward to reading your thoughts and I'll see you in the next installment,

Will

About the Author

For Will Luckman, the journey from award-winning writer to author began on the primary school playground, scribbling poems in his pocket-sized notebook just like any other "cool kid" would have been doing at that age. Now 3 decades later, the former journalist is back on the other side of the teacher's desk, trying to inspire the next generation of "cool kids" to grab a pen and find their own adventure. **The True Tale of Santa the Zombie Slayer** is his debut novel, and from there, anything is possible.

To find out more about Will or to contact him:

- Check out his Amazon author page.

- Email willluckmanwrites@gmail.com

- Join his army of 7 Twitter followers @WLuck-manwrites where he posts at least twice a year.

- Or check out his website. https://willluckmanwrites.wixsite.com/willluckman